Also by Cynthia DeFelice

The Apprenticeship of Lucas Whitaker

Bringing Ezra Back

Death at Devil's Bridge

The Ghost and Mrs. Hobbs

The Ghost of Cutler Creek

The Ghost of Fossil Glen

The Ghost of Poplar Point

Nowhere to Call Home

Under the Same Sky

The Missing Manatee

The Missing Manatee

CYNTHIA DEFELICE

A Sunburst Book
Farrar, Straus and Giroux

Copyright © 2005 by Cynthia C. DeFelice
All rights reserved
Distributed in Canada by Douglas & McIntyre Ltd.
Printed in the United States of America
First edition, 2005
Sunburst edition, 2008
5 7 9 10 8 6 4

Library of Congress Cataloging-in-Publication Data
DeFelice, Cynthia C.
The missing manatee / Cynthia DeFelice.— 1st ed.
p. cm.
Summary: While coping with his parents' separation, eleven-year-old Skeet spends most of spring break in his skiff on a Florida river, where he finds a manatee shot to death and begins looking for the killer.
ISBN-13: 978-0-374-40020-0 (pbk.)
ISBN-10: 0-374-40020-2 (pbk.)
[1. Boats and boating—Fiction. 2. Fishing—Fiction. 3. Family problems—Fiction. 4. Manatees—Fiction. 5. Florida—Fiction. 6. Mystery and detective stories.] I. Title.

PZ7.D3597Mi 2005
[Fic]—dc22

2004050633

For fishing guides Cleve, Pat, Earl, Ben,
Monty, Keith, Mike, Bill, Rick, Eduardo, Oscar,
Allen, Willie, Martin, Dudley, Ken, Tom, and the real,
original Dirty Dan—thanks for all the stories

The Missing Manatee

One

The day I found the dead manatee began badly. I was walking past my mother's bedroom when I overheard her talking on the phone.

"No, Mac. I don't want you to come back. Not now. Not ever," she said.

Mac is my father.

I left the house and got into my skiff and ran a couple of miles out into the Gulf of Mexico, hoping the speed and the salty breeze would blow the words right out of my head. But now, hours later, they continued to cut into the corners of my mind, hard and sharp.

So I decided to call it quits and was heading back upriver when I saw the manatee. It was rocking back and forth like a big, round baby in the gentle waves that lapped the saw grass growing at the edge of a small island.

I guess a tourist might have thought the creature was scratching itself or having a snooze. But I've lived all my eleven years on the river, and I've spent a lot of time watching manatees. Something was wrong with this one.

I cut the engine and glided up to the grass to get a better look. Right away, I could tell it was dead. There wasn't any rotten smell yet, or any swelling, and no gulls or crabs or crows were picking at the flesh, so I knew it hadn't been dead for long.

Looking at that body with all the life gone from it gave me an achy feeling in my chest. Manatees—when they're alive, anyway—are irresistible, the same way puppies and kittens and baby chicks are. They wallow around in the water, too trusting or too lazy to move out of the way of danger. They're so dopey-acting and so homely they're cute.

I read someplace that when the old sailors told of seeing mermaids, they were actually looking at manatees. Which really cracked me up. I mean, a manatee looks kind of like a gigantic dark brown Idaho potato. Or a balloon that got blown up wrong. How those guys imagined that a roly-poly animal with tiny little eyes and a whiskery face was a beautiful woman with a tail—well, if you ask me, they must have been out at sea for a long, *long* time.

I checked the creature's back for propeller scars. Most manatees have slashes across their backs because they don't know enough to swim away from boats. Lots of boaters either don't know that or don't care, so collisions between boats and manatees are pretty common. Not on our river, because it's a manatee refuge, but when the creatures go out into open water, they're almost like sitting ducks.

Yep, I could see that this manatee had had at least one run-in with a propeller, but the scars were old and healed over. I wondered if it might have simply died of old age. I guessed it happened that way sometimes. Was this one old? I didn't know how to tell.

I noticed some streaks of an odd, reddish color swirling in the water. And then I saw a round hole in the back of the creature's head. The red stuff was seeping from it, mixing quickly with the brackish river water. It took a while before I got it: I was looking at blood coming from a bullet hole.

But that didn't make any sense! Manatees are a

protected species. Nobody can hunt them. You can get a stiff fine just for bothering or chasing them. There are bigger fines, even jail sentences, for actually harming or killing one—although I'd never heard of anybody doing that. There was no reason to. The idea of somebody feeling threatened by a manatee and shooting it out of self-defense was so ridiculous it was almost funny. What kind of person would fire a gun at such a harmless animal?

The question made my heart pound unpleasantly, first with anger and then with fear. I looked at the manatee's wound, still bleeding. Whoever had done this might be lurking nearby, watching. He wouldn't want to be discovered, that was for sure. And he had a gun.

Suddenly, I had the feeling that I was being watched. I looked around quickly. To the west the river ran into the gulf, where I'd come from. To the east it headed back inland, toward Chassacoochie Springs, the town where I lived. On both sides of the river were acres and acres of saw grass, mangrove trees, scrubby cedars, and palmettos. There were about a million places for a person to hide, and all I saw were some mullet jumping and an egret preening on the opposite bank.

I took a deep breath to slow the beating of my heart and tried to decide what to do. I knew there was an 800 number to call if you found a dead manatee, or one that was injured, orphaned, or wearing a tag. I'd seen the posters hanging at the marina and in stores hundreds of times, but I'd never memorized the number and, anyway, I didn't have a cell phone.

The radio in my boat wasn't working, either. It needed a new antenna, and I hadn't saved enough yet to get one, although I was getting close. I'd broken the rules that morning, going out in the open ocean without a working radio, and if Mom knew she'd ground me for the rest of my life. If it was up to her, I wouldn't be out alone in the boat in the first place, but Mom realized she couldn't stop me. I'd passed the boating safety course, and had my photo ID card to prove it. Besides, I was Mac's son.

See, Mac—my dad—is a fishing guide. He grew up right in Chassacoochie Springs, and began handling boats when he was six years old. He tried to raise me the same way, and it drove Mom crazy. She was always fussing and calling Mac irresponsible, and he was always telling her to relax, what did she want to do, wrap me in plastic for safekeeping?

That was one of the things they used to argue about, until Mom told Mac to move out three weeks ago. He went down the road a little way to live in a trailer.

"Just for a while," Mom told me, until they "figured things out."

When I asked Mac why he was leaving his own house, why he was leaving *me*, he said he didn't want me to have to listen to any more fighting.

"Then why don't you guys stop?" I said, but he only looked sad, gave me a hug, put a garbage bag with a bunch of his clothes in it in the back of his pickup, and drove off.

Now Mom had decided she didn't want him to come back, and I heard her say it. She hadn't asked me what I wanted. So right then I didn't much care what she would have to say about my being out in the gulf with a busted radio.

Besides, I was looking at a manatee that had to be at least twelve hundred pounds of dead weight. I knew from experience that if I got out of the boat, my feet would sink knee-deep into the wet, oozing mud. If I were lucky, and someone came along and pulled me out, both my sneakers would be sucked under, never to be seen again. But even if I could get out of the skiff, I wasn't strong enough to lift the manatee. And if I *were* able, by some miracle, to get it into the boat, it'd probably sink my skiff. I was going to have to leave it and go tell somebody.

I wasn't worried about finding it again: I knew the river the way I knew my own bedroom. I checked the tide; it was going down. Good—the body wouldn't wash away with high water, and a light wind was pushing it right up against the island.

All of a sudden, I couldn't wait to get away from there. Being alone with that dead body was starting to give me the creeps.

But when I came back less than an hour later with a deputy from the sheriff's department, the manatee was gone.

Two

"It was right there," I said.

Deputy Sheriff Earl Wells looked at the little island, empty of everything except a cormorant drying its wings in the sun, then at me. "You sure it was dead, Skeet?" he asked. "Maybe it was just relaxing, you know how they do. Maybe it swam off."

I shook my head. "It was *dead*, Earl." Earl played cards on Tuesday nights with Mac, so I'd known him my whole life. I tried to remember to call him Deputy when he was on duty, but I usually forgot. "It was right *there*," I repeated, pointing.

There was silence for a second as we both stared at the deserted stretch of mud and saw grass. Then I said, "Wait a second. Look! Somebody was here!

Check out those marks in the mud. Like something was dragged. Whoever did it tried to smooth it over, see?"

"I'll be doggoned," said Earl, leaning down and peering at the mud, which had obviously been disturbed, then roughly smoothed over.

"Somebody came after I left and *took* it," I said. "I don't believe this."

I stared at Earl, who always looked to me as if he had a fishing bobber in his throat, the way his Adam's apple stuck out and moved up and down when he talked. "Had to have a boat," he observed. "Nobody could carry a thing like that. Couldn't have dragged it farther up on shore without sinking."

I was still so stunned by the manatee's disappearance, I just nodded in agreement.

"I'll be doggoned," Earl said again, straightening up. He shaded his eyes with his hands and scanned the horizon, but there were no boats in sight. "Could have done it alone, though, if he tied a rope around it and towed it. It'd float," he went on thoughtfully. "Could have cut it loose anywhere out there," he added, gesturing with his arm to indicate the miles and miles of mangrove swamp crisscrossed by hundreds of little channels and creeks, not to mention the whole Gulf of Mexico.

"But *why*?" I blurted out. "Why not just leave the body? Why go to the trouble of getting rid of it?"

I shivered as a possible answer occurred to me. The killer *had* been watching when I discovered his dirty work. And he knew that if I went and reported it and the body was examined, there might be a clue that would reveal who he was.

Earl swallowed, and the fishing bobber bobbed. "I believe you saw a manatee here, Skeet," he began, sounding apologetic. "And if you say it was dead, I guess it was. But, I gotta ask—are you sure you were looking at a bullet hole?"

"Well, *yeah*. What else could it be?"

"I don't know. An ear, maybe?" Earl scratched his own ear speculatively.

Living near the refuge the way we did, we'd studied manatees in school, and I knew a lot about them. "Manatees' ears are little openings up near their eyes," I said. "This was farther back. And there was only one. It was round. And it was bleeding."

Earl nodded again, staring out toward the horizon. "Just the one hole?" he asked.

"Yes," I answered, not sure what he was getting at.

"Entrance wound, no exit wound," he said thoughtfully. "So the bullet—"

"Is still in there!" I finished excitedly. "That's why he wanted to hide the body. If you had the bullet, you could figure out who did it!"

"Not necessarily," Earl corrected. "But it would sure help."

We were quiet for a minute, thinking about it. "Hard to understand, though, why anybody'd want to do such a thing," Earl said, shaking his head. "They're harmless critters, far as I know." He paused, then mused, "Never heard of anybody eating the meat."

"Yuck," I said, not even wanting to think about it. Eating a manatee would be like eating somebody's pet dog or cat.

"And I don't believe I've ever seen a trophy manatee head hangin' on the wall of anybody's den," Earl drawled, looking at me with a sideways grin.

Imagining it, I grinned back. But then I pictured the lifeless body again, and felt the smile slide off my face.

"The only people I've ever heard complain about the manatees are some of the fishing guides," Earl said thoughtfully. "Not Mac, but some of the others."

"Yeah, I've heard 'em, too," I said. "They hate having to slow down when they go through the refuge area. It takes them longer to get where they're going, and cuts down on their fishing time."

Earl laughed and said, "You know what Dirty Dan calls manatees, don't you?"

I shook my head. Dirty Dan was a friend of Earl's and Mac's.

"Live speed bumps," said Earl with a chortle.

Ordinarily, I'd probably have laughed, too, but not right then. "He doesn't mean anything by it," I said.

"Nah," Earl agreed. "He's only griping 'cause he likes to run his boat flat out." After a minute he said, "About the only thing I can imagine is that some good old boys, or maybe some teenage kids, got drunked up and stupid."

I nodded. It was a possibility. "So how are we going to catch 'em?" I asked.

"Hold on now, Skeet," Earl said. "I don't think we'll be sending out the posse on this."

"We won't?" I said, feeling confused. Did Earl mean we were going to go after the guy ourselves? I felt first thrilled, then terrified, at the prospect.

But Earl said, "First thing we'll do is go back and report it to Fish and Wildlife. Ordinarily, they'd be the ones to investigate if somebody killed or even hurt a manatee. If we had the body, they'd probably send it to St. Pete for study. But—" He shrugged, holding out his empty hands.

"But what?"

"Without a body, there isn't much to investigate. They might even take the position that without a body, there's no proof there was a crime."

"But there *was* a body!" I protested.

"I know, I know," Earl said soothingly. "It's too bad it up and disappeared. What I'm saying, Skeet, is that law-enforcement folks are busy. This isn't going to be real high up on their list of priorities."

I couldn't believe this. "It's because I'm a kid, isn't it?" I muttered. "Nobody ever listens to kids."

"It's not that, Skeet," Earl said. His Adam's apple bobbed and he said softly, "I'm just trying to be realistic here."

"But somebody shot a manatee!" I said. "It's against the law, right? You think he should just get away with it? That's not fair!"

"No, all I'm saying—"

"It's not right, Earl."

Earl sighed. "I hear you, Skeet, but—"

I interrupted again. I couldn't help it. "I should have stayed here until somebody else came along in a boat," I said in disgust. "Then we'd have the proof." Even as I said it, I remembered the fear I'd felt there with the dead creature at my feet, imagining the killer nearby.

"Listen to me, Skeet," Earl was saying. "You did the right thing. Think about it. Whoever did this was near enough to take the body away before we arrived, and we got out here pretty quick. I'm glad you weren't here for long, especially if it *was* a bunch of drunks that did the shooting."

Maybe Earl was right, but I figured he was just trying to make me feel better.

"We'll go back and make our report," he said. "And who knows? Maybe I'm wrong and they'll pursue this thing. But don't count on it, Skeet. We don't have any evidence, and the departments are all pretty strapped right now."

"Okay," I said, even though it wasn't okay at all. Earl was making it sound as if I was supposed to go back, make a stupid report, and wait to see what happened, which would be nothing. But I wanted to know who killed the manatee and hid the body, and why. Whoever it was ought to be caught and punished, plain and simple.

I sighed, and stepped back into the patrol boat.

Three

Even with the dead manatee on my mind, I enjoyed the ride back upriver in the sheriff's boat. Earl zoomed through the curves and bends of the river, going close to sixty miles an hour. That felt really fast compared to my skiff, which maxed out at around twenty-five. He throttled down to idle speed when we reached the upper section of the river, where the manatees' refuge began. This was the section Earl and I had been talking about, the section that irritated some of the guides who had fast boats and wanted to use them.

It was April, and there were still about two hundred manatees around. They arrived in October to spend the winter, and some never left when spring came. They were eating and swimming and hanging out in the warm water coming from the spring at the river's source. We passed a bunch of them, lolling contentedly. Which is what a manatee *should* be doing, I thought, not getting ditched someplace with a bullet in its head.

We passed other boats, too. The river was busy with tourists who came every winter, like the manatees, looking for warmth and relaxation. A good number of the boats belonged to local folks, who recognized either Earl or me and waved as we passed them.

It was spring break, so I wasn't surprised to see some kids from school casting off the pier at the public dock when we idled by. I waved to my friend Lenny. Watching his face as he waved back, I could tell he was wondering what the heck I was doing out with the sheriff's department.

Then I looked upriver and called to Earl above the engine noise, "Hey, there's Mac!"

Earl knew I called my father Mac, but it confused most people. "He's your *dad*," kids would say. "Why don't you call him *Dad*?"

I'd always shrug and say, "Nicknames run in our family." Which was true. I was called Skeet, short for Skeeter, which was short for mosquito. That's what Mac claimed I looked like when I was born. "Why, he's no bigger than a skeeter," he said when he first saw me, or so I've been told.

I've been trying my best to grow ever since.

Nobody ever calls me Russell Waters, Jr., which is my real name, except for teachers on the first day of school. Then I set them straight. And nobody calls my father Russ or Russell Sr., either, not even Mom. He's Mac.

"You want to stop?" Earl asked me.

Since he'd been gone, it seemed I was always wishing I could see Mac about one thing or another. I could pick up the phone anytime I wanted to, or ride my bike the couple of blocks to his place, but it wasn't the same as having him at home. Right then I wanted to tell him about the manatee in the worst way, but he had a client. Mac had the guy in a good position for casting shrimp to redfish or trout. The guy was standing in the bow, gazing at the water so intently he reminded me of a great blue heron waiting to pounce on a minnow. He looked as if he took his fishing seriously.

"Naw," I said. "I don't want to bother him."

Earl nodded. He knew the fishing-guide business as well as I did. Keeping the clients happy came first.

When we pulled into Larry's Marina, Larry himself was pumping gas into a pontoon barge filled with partying vacationers. He gave Earl and me a tired wave as we passed by. The money he made during tourist season was most likely what kept his business going, but he liked to act as though the extra work was killing him.

I helped Earl tie up the boat in its slip. As we headed for his patrol car, Blink came out of the shop toward me, grinning from ear to ear, followed by his mangy, flea-bitten dog, named Blinky. Blink —the boy, not the dog—was Dirty Dan's son.

Dan's official title was Dirty Dan the Tarpon Man. He was the best tarpon fisherman in these parts, probably in the whole state of Florida, maybe even the entire world. He was also Mac's and Earl's poker-playing friend, and my hero. I didn't know which of Dirty Dan's four wives was Blink's mother. They had all left Dirty Dan because of his single-minded devotion to tarpon fishing, but Blink stayed on. I guessed he always would.

I called Blink a *boy*, but once I asked Mac how

old Blink was, and I was astonished when he said he reckoned Blink was around thirty. The thing is, something was wrong with Blink when he was born. No matter how old his body got, in his head he'd never be any older than five or maybe six, and that's how he acted.

If I ever knew his real name, I've forgotten it. Everybody called him Blink, even Dirty Dan. It was on account of his eyes, which were always opening real wide, then shutting tight, then opening again, all on their own.

He was the one who named the dog Blinky. Maybe it was the best name he could think of, or maybe he knew he and that dog would get so close, you might as well call one as call the other. Anyway, Blink loved that dog like nobody's business, even though Blinky was the most pathetic-looking creature you can imagine, with matted, stinky fur, insect-bite sores, and his tail broken so it hung at a right angle halfway down. That didn't stop him from smiling and wagging at everybody he saw, though. I never knew a dog could smile, until I met Blinky.

Blink and Blinky were always at the marina. Dirty Dan kept a little pop-up camper around behind the parking lot, and that's where the three of them lived. It suited them fine. Blink hung around at the marina throwing a ball for Blinky and doing simple odd jobs for Larry sometimes, and all Dan had to do was roll out of bed and he was tarpon fishing.

So Blink came grinning and Blinky came smiling and wagging toward me across the scrubby grass of the marina's picnic area. I knew exactly what Blink was going to do, and sure enough he reached into his pocket, took out a quarter, and said, "Wanna flip, Skeet?"

Ordinarily, I'd say sure and Blink and I would play his favorite game, one that he never seemed to grow tired of. It was funny, but I never got tired of playing it with him, I guess because he got such a big kick out of it. But this time I was in a hurry, all puffed up with the importance of having an official police report to make.

"Can't now, Blink," I said quickly. "I got something I got to do."

The corners of his mouth drooped and his eyes opened and closed quickly. "Uh-oh, Skeet's mad. Don't be mad, Skeet. I'm sorry, Blink's real sorry. Don't be mad—"

He looked ready to cry, and I felt like a real crumb. "Aw, Blink, I'm not mad," I said. "It's just that I gotta go with Earl and—never mind. Give me the quarter. Let's flip."

At that, his face lit up as if I'd given him a present or something. He handed me the quarter and I made a fist and positioned the quarter on the top of my thumbnail. "What'll it be?" I asked.

Blink screwed up his face as if in thought and finally called, "Heads!"

I popped my thumb and flipped the quarter into the air, caught it, and slapped my open palm onto the back of my other hand. Blink and Blinky both watched me intently. Slowly, with a dramatic flourish, I removed the top hand, revealing the quarter. Blink peered over to look.

"Heads!" he crowed joyfully. "I win! Do it again, Skeet!"

I was already positioning the quarter for the next try. "What'll it be?"

Again, Blink squinched up his face, but I knew what he was going to say this time.

"Tails!"

I flipped, paused, and uncovered the coin. Blink looked. It was heads. His face fell into a tragic mask. He was as sad each time he was wrong as he was happy when he was right. "Oh, no. I lose. Do it again, Skeet!"

I flipped the quarter a few more times until he'd called it right twice in a row. Then I handed it back, saying, as I always did, "That's it, Blink. You're getting too good."

He smiled happily and repeated, "I'm getting too good." Carefully, he returned the quarter to his pocket, saying, as he always did, "I'll save it for another day. Right, Skeet?"

"That's right. Save it for another day."

"Bye, Skeet."

"See ya, Blink."

I ran to catch up with Earl. He was waiting beside the police car talking to Larry, who was on his way into the marina's office with the pontoon boat driver's credit card.

"Sounds like you've had yourself quite a morning, Skeeter," Larry observed as I walked up to them.

"Yeah, I guess," I answered.

"Terrible thing," Larry said. "But I can see where it'd be tough to investigate without any evidence."

I scowled. Everybody agreed it was a terrible thing, so how come nobody except me wanted to do anything about it?

"Well, I gotta go take this gentleman's money," Larry said, holding up the credit card. "I'll be seein' you."

I was pretty discouraged when I got into the patrol car with Earl. He was quiet on the way to the station, and that made me feel a little guilty. If he was right and the sheriff and the Fish and Wildlife people weren't going to work too hard on the case, it wasn't his fault.

"Thanks for going out there with me, Earl," I said in a low voice.

He was quiet for another minute. Then he nodded and said, "I want you to know I'm gonna try my best to get the boss fired up about this, Skeet. C'mon, let's go see him."

But the sheriff wasn't there. Earl helped me fill out a report about what I'd seen. Then he drove me back to the marina, where I'd left my bike. I rode home, passing the trailer where Mac lived since he'd left. Left permanently, it now appeared.

Mom was at work at the Quik-Save, where she

was manager of the movie-rental department. It seemed like a pretty good job, but she was always saying she wanted a better life for me.

"What do you mean, better?" I used to ask.

"Better than *this*," she'd say, throwing her arms out to indicate not only her job but our house, the town of Chassacoochie Springs, our whole lives.

"But what's wrong with *this*?" I'd say, her words making me feel puzzled and hurt. I liked our lives the way they were, at least the way they used to be before Mac had to go.

Mom would get a sort of faraway, dreamy look on her face and say, "Oh, Skeet, there's so much more out there. Why, you can be anything you want."

"I want to be a fishing guide."

"Oh, no, Skeet. No. You could be a rocket scientist, a doctor, maybe a researcher who discovers a cure for some horrible disease . . ."

"Come on, Mom," I'd tease. "With a last name like Waters, what else can I be but a guide, like Mac?"

She'd tease back: "Why, you could be a scientist, like Jacques Cousteau. A marine biologist. Or . . ."

She'd pause to think, then add, "Or a swimming pool manufacturer. Or a cruise ship captain. Think of that! You'd get to travel all over the world."

But I didn't want to be any of those things, and kidding around didn't change that. I wanted to be a fishing guide like Mac, and a legendary fisherman like Dirty Dan. I mean, how cool would it be to be known as "the Tarpon Man"?

"Why don't *you* do that stuff, if you think it sounds so great?" I'd ask.

And Mom would look sad and say, "I made my choice when I married your father. It's too late for me. But, Skeet, you have your whole life ahead of you."

Yeah, I always wanted to say, *and it's* my *life, not yours.* Lately I'd stopped talking about how I planned to be a great fisherman and a guide, because I didn't want to see the disappointment on her face. I knew what she thought of fishing guides, and I didn't want to get her started on her speech about their "deviant lifestyle." How they got up at four in the morning and fell asleep in front of the TV at six o'clock at night, not leaving much time for what she called "quality family life." How lots of them drank too much. How they made lousy husbands and fathers because they cared more about fish than about their families. How there must be some kind of wild gene that caused them to spend day after day in a boat under the blazing sun with clients who half the time turned out to be jerks, hoping to stick a hook in a fish that they ended up releasing after they'd landed it anyway.

And how she sure hoped her son hadn't inherited that wild gene.

Man.

So anyway, Mom was still at work when I got home, but Memaw—she's my grandmother—was in the living room sitting at the sewing machine, stitching some glittery silver stuff onto her favorite denim cowgirl shirt. She looked up at me and smiled. I could tell right away that she was up to something.

"Skeeter, there's a big karaoke contest tonight at the River Haven Grill, and I aim to sing in it. You and your mama are comin' to cheer me on!"

Four

Memaw hogged the bathroom for about an hour, taking a long bath and fooling with her hair. Before she came out she called to Mom and me, "Don't you two look yet. I want you to see me with my whole outfit on, so you can get the full effect."

Mom shook her head and gave me a look and a little smile as if to say, Here she goes again. For a mother and daughter, Mom and Memaw were pretty different. It was weird, but I thought Mac and Memaw were more alike. Mom was always saying Memaw ought to act her age. Memaw said why should she, with Mom acting enough like an old stick-in-the-mud for both of them.

Once when they didn't know I was listening, Mom said Memaw was embarrassing. Memaw said she couldn't understand why Mom had to be the ant in the lemonade at every picnic lunch. I tried to stay out of it, but it seemed to me that Memaw was having a lot more fun than Mom. And anyway, Memaw never embarrassed me.

A couple of minutes later, Memaw hollered from the bedroom, "I'm coming out. You ready?"

"We're ready, Memaw," I hollered back. "Bring it on!"

The door opened and Memaw stood in front of us with her hands on her hips, posing like a movie star. Then she threw her arms out and spun around, so we could get the whole picture. Her blond hair was piled up high in loops and curls, held with sparkly silver-and-blue clips. She was wearing her denim shirt, all decorated with silver fringe and sequins. Her jeans had a row of sequins down the side of each leg, which she must have just sewn on, and she was wearing a belt with a big silver heart-shaped buckle. Around her neck she'd tied a red cowgirl bandanna, and she was wearing her favorite red cowgirl boots.

"Well?" she asked. "What do you think?"

"Wow, Memaw," I said. "You look like a singer on TV."

"Not too bad for an old grandma, am I?"

"No way. You look great."

"Thank you, darlin'." She gave me a dazzling red-lipstick smile. Then, snapping her fingers with one hand and holding a pretend microphone in the other, she launched into a song I'd heard her practicing around the house. It was called "These Boots Are Made for Walking."

When she started singing, Mom clapped and I stood up and cheered and let out my loudest whistle. "Go, Memaw! Knock 'em dead!"

After a minute or two, she got to the part of the song where she stops singing and sort of talks to her boots, telling them to start walking. At that, Memaw held her chin up real high, pumped her arms back and forth, and marched in place, stomping her feet like anything. It was pretty spectacular.

When she'd finished, I said, "You got that contest won, Memaw. No point in the rest of 'em even showin' up!"

"You really think so, Skeeter?" she said, giving me a big, perfumey hug. "I hope you're right. I'd dearly love to win that home karaoke setup they're giving out for the prize."

Mom made a little choking sound in her throat right then, and I could tell she wasn't exactly thrilled about the prospect of Memaw practicing new songs, with musical backup, right there in the living room.

I said, "That'll be great, Memaw." And I meant it, too.

We got to the River Haven Grill at six o'clock. The contest didn't start until seven, but Memaw said she wanted to get a good seat and check out the competition. Mom and I ordered burgers, but Memaw said her stomach was too jittery to eat. She ordered a Lone Star beer to "get in the mood." I guess that's what cowgirls like to drink.

We sat on the outside patio where the contest was going to be held and watched people as they drifted in. Memaw checked everybody over with an eagle eye.

"Don't worry, Memaw," I told her. "Don't any of 'em look half as good as you."

"Thanks, darlin'," she said. "But you can't always tell by lookin'. Sometimes a dull brown bird can make a mighty sweet song."

Well, I guess. But still, I felt sure Memaw would win.

Then I heard Mom take a sudden, sharp breath. I turned in the direction she was looking, and saw Mac walk onto the patio with Earl and Dirty Dan.

"There's Mac!" I said.

"And look who he dragged in with him," Mom said drily. "The aptly named Dirty Dan."

It killed me that Mom didn't like Dan. She called him "shiftless" because he didn't have a real job. I'd tried to explain to her that he didn't *need* a job. He made money at poker and by winning tarpon tournaments. If he was strapped for cash, he'd take a client out tarpon fishing for pay, but mostly he just fished for himself.

Mom thought even fishing guides who worked regularly were shiftless, so her opinion of Dan was right down there in the mud with the crabs. I guess Dan's four wives probably agreed with Mom, now that I thought about it. But I didn't care. Dan was a lot of the things I hoped to be someday. And, anyway, he was Mac's and Memaw's friend.

There was a famous story about Dan I never got tired of hearing. It always came with a warning:

Don't even think of trying this yourself. One day when he was out fishing, Dan hooked up a giant tarpon. He fought it and fought it for about three hours. Finally, when it was getting tired, a hammerhead shark showed up and started circling around. They do that sometimes, when they sense a fish is in trouble. They figure on getting themselves an easy meal.

But there was no way Dirty Dan the Tarpon Man was going to give up his record tarpon to a shark, no sir. So he jumped right into the water, which was only a couple of feet deep, with his rod in one hand and his fish club in the other.

Some people think hammerheads are kind of a joke because they look so silly. I mean, they have those weird rectangle-shaped heads that look like they were put on sideways, and their eyes are way out on the ends. But they are seriously scary predators, with huge mouths and rows and rows of real sharp teeth. They get big, too.

Anyway, Dan stood right in the water and whacked that ten-foot-long monster on the head every time it came near his fish! After a while, the shark gave up and swam away. Each time I heard the story, I had to laugh, picturing that shark swimming off, wondering in its prehistoric little brain, What the heck is going on?

Dirty Dan landed his record tarpon and there wasn't a bite missing. He wasn't called the Tarpon Man for nothing.

"I'm going to go say hi, okay?" I asked Mom.

"Sure, honey." She smiled at me when she said it, but it was one of those forced smiles.

I hated times like this, when I wanted to be with both Mom and Mac like before, and the only way I could do that was to split myself down the middle. "I'll be back in a sec," I said, and raced over to where Mac and his friends were taking seats across the patio.

"Hey there, Skeet," said Mac, grabbing me in a bear hug. "I hear you got yourself deputized today. Or were you just trying to give Earl here a lesson on how to run a boat? Lord knows, he could use it."

"You hear that, Skeet?" said Earl, shaking his head sadly. "You'd think your daddy would know better than to smart-mouth an officer of the law."

Dirty Dan said, "I believe there's strict penalties for sassing a deputy. Isn't that right, Officer Earl?"

"Yessir," said Earl. "*Very* strict."

Pointing his finger at Mac, Earl said, "Looks like you're gonna have to bring the food *and* the beer Tuesday night, old buddy."

"No problem," Mac answered cheerfully. "You two just bet the way you always do, and I'll have double my money back before eight o'clock." Then he looked at me and said, "Earl told me how you found that manatee this morning."

I nodded, and looked hopefully at Earl, but he shook his head. "No news yet."

"Strange the way it wasn't there when you went back," Mac went on. "How do you figure a thing like that?"

I shrugged and said, "I don't know, but I'd sure like to see the person who did it go to jail." Then, grinning at Dirty Dan, I imitated his deep voice and added, "I believe there's strict penalties for that."

I expected Dan to come back with a wisecrack, but instead he said, "I believe I heard Mac say you're on vacation from school. Is that right, Skeet?"

"Yeah."

"Have you caught yourself a tarpon on a fly yet?"

"No," I admitted. "I've caught a couple on bait, though."

Dan snorted. I knew what he thought about bait fishing for tarpon. To Dan, the only way to take one of the big, beautiful silver beauties was on a fly. "You want to come tarpon fishing with me some day this week?" he asked.

Did I want to go tarpon fishing with Dirty Dan, the Tarpon Man? Do fish swim? I looked at Mac. Seeing the hesitation on his face, I knew what he was thinking: Mom wouldn't approve. But Mac also knew how badly I wanted to catch a tarpon on a fly, how many times I'd tried and failed. He'd taken me out a lot, but Mac was primarily a bait fisherman. Dirty Dan was a fly fisherman exclusively, and he was the best. With Dan, I had a real chance. Mac understood that.

I willed him to say yes. What he said was, "I'll have to talk to your mom about it, Skeet."

Right. Mac couldn't make his own decisions about me the way he used to. He had to talk over every little thing with Mom. I scowled in frustration.

Mac gave my arm a reassuring squeeze. "Don't you worry. I think it'll be all right."

Turning to Dan I said, "Thanks! I really hope I can come."

"If your mother says it's okay, you come to Mac's Tuesday night," said Dan. "After I whup these two at cards, we'll check your gear and tie up some flies. Wednesday morning, we'll go out, catch you a silver king. Deal?"

"Deal!" I said.

Just then, music blared over the sound system, and the deejay stepped behind the podium and began fiddling with the microphone, which let out a loud squeal.

"It's the karaoke contest," I said. "I better go back. Memaw's singing."

Dan's face broke into a big grin. "Oooweee!" he said. "*This* I want to hear."

Mac and the others all turned to the table where Mom and Memaw were sitting, waved, and smiled. Memaw waved back gaily and Mom wiggled her hand halfheartedly.

"Go on," said Mac, and he gave me another hug. "Don't worry, I'll talk to her," he said softly.

"Thanks, Mac," I said. I wanted to ask him what Mom had said to him on the phone that morning, so he could tell me I'd heard wrong or it was all a misunderstanding and he was coming back soon. But this wasn't the right time or place to talk. It was never the right time or place anymore. Feeling a familiar lump rising in my throat, I swallowed it quickly and said, "See ya."

The deejay was explaining that the winner of the contest would be the person who got the loudest applause after singing. "So clap real loud for your favorite, ladies and gentlemen," he told us, "and my state-of-the-art, scientifically accurate applause-o-meter will record the level." He held up something that looked like half a clock with numbers on it from one to ten, and a big arrow, and everybody cheered.

"Let's begin now, and find out who will be the lucky guy or gal to win this fantastic home karaoke machine!" He pulled a slip of paper from a box and said, "Please welcome our first contestant, Mrs. Arlene Kimball, who will be singing 'Proud Mary.' "

"Good," Memaw said. "I didn't want to go first." She gave me a wink and added, "The darker it gets, the better I'll look up there."

Arlene Kimball did an okay job, I guess, but I whispered to Memaw, "You'd give that 'rollin' on the river' part a lot more pizzazz, wouldn't you, Memaw?"

"Shush, now," she said, but she was smiling, and she gave my hand a little squeeze.

The deejay cupped his hand to his ear to listen for the applause, then moved the meter to 4. Arlene smiled kind of weakly, and sat down next to a guy I figured was Mr. Kimball. He'd been cheering his head off anyway.

The next lady sang a slow, sad song about the morning light coming after the dark, dark night. Her voice got real high and quivery toward the end, and, with a tragic expression to go with the mournful words, she clutched at her throat with one hand and dropped her head, to show she was plain wrung out from the emotion of it all.

I rolled my eyes at Memaw and she laughed. There was some polite clapping, and the meter registered 2.

A few of the singers who followed were pretty good. We got a bad scare from a husband-and-wife team who scored an 8, and a young guy who couldn't sing for anything, but had a lot of friends who clapped and cheered and whistled and stomped his score up to a 9.

When it was Memaw's turn, I was suddenly nervous as all get-out. But she walked up there as if she owned the place. No embarrassed looks or bashful giggles for Memaw. The minute she started snapping her fingers, I noticed everybody in the place sat up and paid real close attention. When she got to the part where she sang, "One of these days these boots are gonna walk all over *you*," she narrowed her eyes and pointed out into the crowd, and it was clear to everyone that Memaw was no one to mess with. Then during the talking part she made her voice real low and dangerous, and the music got spiky and jazzy. Memaw started her boots marching and the crowd went crazy. When she was finished, Dirty Dan ran right up onstage and gave her a big hug and a kiss, lifting her right off the ground to do it.

Well, I probably don't have to tell the rest. Memaw scored a 10, and the deejay said she'd have gotten an 11 if the meter had had one. There were a few more contestants after that, and I felt sorry for them having to follow Memaw. It was as if they had the stuffing knocked out of them before they even started.

Mac and Earl came over to congratulate Memaw afterwards, and they helped Dirty Dan and me carry the karaoke machine out to Mom's car. Mom walked with us, while Memaw stayed to collect a few last compliments from her admirers.

Mac told Mom he needed to speak to her, so I got into the car, and they walked off into the parking lot a ways.

I watched as they talked. I couldn't hear their exact words, but I didn't need to. I'd heard them argue so many times about what I was and wasn't allowed to do that I could pretty much imagine the conversation.

Mom shook her head, and Mac talked some more. I crossed my fingers, whispering over and over, "Please let me go, please, please, please let me go."

Then Mom frowned and folded her arms over her chest.

"Please, please, please," I murmured, while she held on to her elbows and stared up into the sky, looking annoyed. It seemed like a long time.

Finally, Mom looked at Mac and said loud enough so I could hear it from the car, "All right.

But you're in charge. If that boy comes back with one hair on his head harmed, you and Dan are both going to have to answer to me."

Mac nodded and said a few more words, then Mom was walking toward the car. Mac headed back inside, but first he turned to me with the grin that made him look like a big, naughty kid, and gave me a thumbs-up.

I could hardly believe it. I was going tarpon fishing with Dirty Dan.

Five

I had a hard time getting to sleep that night, with my mind flying back and forth between Mom and Mac, the prospect of fishing with Dan, and the dead manatee. I kept trying to figure out who the killer might be and what he looked like, and how the whole thing had happened and why.

Then I'd picture a scene in which I had a huge tarpon on the line. Sometimes I landed it; sometimes I did something wrong and it got away.

When I finally got to sleep, I had some very weird dreams. The manatee killer appeared. As I fought him, he turned into a giant hammerhead shark, laughing at me, his big mouth open to show rows of sharp teeth.

The shark turned into my English teacher, Mr. Giordano, who had given us a writing assignment to do during our break. We'd all groaned, and he had tried to make it better by saying, "It only has to be a first draft. And I think you're going to like this one. I want you to write about a pet peeve."

My buddy Lenny had raised his hand and said, "How about if your pet peeve is having to do writing assignments over vacation?"

All the kids had laughed. Mr. Giordano had just smiled and said, "Fine. Then write about it. But let me feel the passion in your words."

I'd forgotten about the assignment, but I guess my dream brain hadn't. I had a very passionate nightmare about staring at a blank sheet of paper for hours with no clue of what to say.

Then I dreamed I was outside Mom's bedroom hearing those words: "I don't want you to come back. Not now. Not ever."

I was relieved when Memaw knocked on my door in the morning, calling, "Rise and shine!"

"Come on in," I croaked.

She peered in, her eyes bright and wide awake.

"Come on and get up, Skeeter," she said. "I'm real hungry after last night's excitement. We're going to Sunday brunch at Fat Boy's to celebrate—my treat!"

I knew there was no point in getting between Memaw and a meal at Fat Boy's Bar-B-Q, so I dragged myself out of bed, brushed my teeth, and got dressed in a groggy daze. I sat in the backseat on the way to the restaurant, and dozed until we got there.

Once we were seated in our booth, it was plain that while Memaw was still fired up over her karaoke triumph, Mom was in a very different mood. She looked around the room, sighed, and said gloomily, "I'd like to pack up and move far away from here."

That woke me up. I didn't like the sound of it at all. I didn't want to move anywhere; I liked it fine where we were.

Mom was too busy being bummed out to notice my distress. "Then I think, where would I go at this point in my life?" she went on. "Where else could I go where I'd be the best-looking woman in town, simply because I have all my teeth and weigh less than two hundred pounds?"

Sunday is all-you-can-eat day at Fat Boy's, and there were a lot of folks taking what you might call full advantage of the offer. As I looked around the place, I thought Mom might have a point.

But Memaw wasn't having any of it. "*I* live in this town, and I'll have you know I weigh the same as the day I was married," she said haughtily. She reached up to pat her hair. It was the same blond color it was when she got married, too, thanks to the smelly foam she put on it every month.

I smiled, noticing that Memaw didn't say anything about having all her teeth. I'd seen what she called her "partial" in a glass by her bed plenty of times.

"And anyway," Mom said, "who cares what I look like? The only eligible bachelors around here are fishing guides, and I made that mistake once already."

Oh, boy. I hoped she wouldn't get going on that subject. I never knew what to do when she started. I didn't want to argue with her, but at the same time, I always felt as though I should defend Mac. Besides, what was she doing talking about eligible bachelors?

Luckily, Memaw spoke before Mom could get

up a head of steam. "Well, I don't worry about such things myself," she said, picking up her menu and studying it with a hungry eye.

"That's fine for you," Mom pointed out. "You're not looking for a husband."

"Who says I'm not?" Memaw asked indignantly, giving me a sly wink. "There were a number of gentlemen last evening who seemed interested in the position, if I do say so myself."

But I was still trying to take in what Mom had said. "Are *you*?" I asked her, and I was embarrassed to hear my voice come out kind of squeaky. "Looking for a husband, I mean?"

She blushed, as if just realizing what she'd said. "Oh, Skeet, no. Not really. But, well, your father and I—"

"I know," I interrupted. "You kicked him out for good." I was surprised and a little scared by how angry I sounded.

Mom looked surprised, too. Then her face darkened. "Has he been talking to you about this? Because he promised me—"

I interrupted again. "No, it wasn't him. It was you. On the phone yesterday morning."

Her face looked crumply for a minute. Then she

straightened up and brushed the hair away from her forehead. "I'm sorry you heard that, Skeeter. Your father and I intended to talk to you about this together. And we will, honey. Don't you worry about it right now, okay?"

It was a ridiculous thing to say, and I didn't answer. What was I supposed to say? *Sure, Mom, okay. I won't worry about a thing.*

"As for that business about looking for a husband," she went on, "well, I was only talking, honey. I'm sorry. Don't pay any attention to me."

"We're not," Memaw said firmly. "You can sit there in a blue funk if you want to, but Skeet and I are here to celebrate, right, Skeeter?"

"Right," I mumbled, opening my menu and burying my face in it.

We were quiet until the waitress came to take our order. After she left, there was another long, uneasy silence, until finally Memaw said, "I declare! If I'd known you were going to be such party poopers, I'd have come by myself. I'd be better off trying to celebrate with that napkin holder than with you two sad sacks. Maybe I'll just move over to the next table and see if those nice folks would like to hear about my karaoke machine."

Mom sighed deeply and gazed into space. But I felt bad for Memaw. I was trying to think of something to liven up the party when I remembered I hadn't told Mom and Memaw about the manatee, what with the karaoke contest and all. So while we waited for our food to come, I did, leaving out the part about the radio being busted. Luckily, Mom didn't think to ask why I hadn't called for help.

She and Memaw were both real interested, and asked all kinds of questions, most of which I didn't know the answers to, such as what was going to happen next. And the one everyone seemed to ask: What kind of awful person would do such a thing?

Memaw was especially outraged. "I swear," she said. "If that isn't the flat-out meanest thing I can think of." Her blue eyes flashed.

I had to smile, thinking I wouldn't want to be the killer if Memaw ever discovered him. Especially if she had her boots on.

Anyway, after talking about the manatee, I began looking around the restaurant, playing a game, checking out each man to see if he looked like the manatee-killer type. I had the feeling that if I saw him, I'd know somehow. If you were a bad guy like that, wouldn't it show? The people at Fat Boy's might have been above average in size, but they didn't appear very menacing.

I started thinking about what I'd do after brunch, and decided I'd go out in my skiff. I could pick up some extra money by catching baitfish and selling them to Larry, who would sell them to fishermen. I really did want to get the cash I needed to get a new antenna for my radio, the sooner the better.

"Mom? Can I—" She shot me a look. Mom was determined not to have me grow up "ignorant," which was what she called it when people said "ain't" for "isn't," and "can" when they meant "may." Exactly as she was determined that I have "a better life" than hers or Mac's.

She had so many plans for me, sometimes it made me tired. She was always sending away for college brochures and reminding me I had to keep my grades up so I'd be able to get in. Then she'd say I had to do well in college, too, so I could go on to graduate school, so I'd be able to get some fancy job she dreamed of for me.

I'd remind her that I was only eleven years old, and that my grades *were* good, and that the job I wanted was to be a fishing guide. She'd say I was too young to know what I wanted, which really ticked me off.

I didn't want a different life; I wanted our old life, the one that used to be hers and Mac's and Memaw's and mine.

I corrected myself. "*May* I go out in the boat when we get back?"

She cocked her head to the side, raised her eyebrow, and asked, "You're going to leave this manatee business to the police—or the wildlife people, or to whoever's responsible—right?"

In a way, it was kind of flattering that Mom thought I might be going out to investigate on my own. I shrugged. "It's not like I have much choice," I answered, which was true and not true at the same time.

"Well, then, I don't see why you can't go," Mom said. She smiled. "You're on vacation, after all." She paused, then asked, "Do you have any homework?"

"Not much," I said. "Just a paper for English."

"Have you started it?"

"No. But I still have lots of time."

"Okay, then. But when you go out in the boat, remember the rules."

Was she kidding? I knew the rules by heart. I

had to wear a life jacket whenever I was in a boat by myself and whenever any boat I was in was moving. Also, I had to tell somebody approximately where I was going and, I thought guiltily, I had to have a radio or some way to call for help.

Knowing the rules didn't mean I always followed them.

"I will," I said. "I'll just be in the river today, no farther than the mouth."

She nodded. Then she added in a warning tone, "I expect you to follow the rules when you're out with Dan on Wednesday, too."

It was the first we'd spoken about that. "I will," I repeated. "And thanks for letting me go."

"Your father assured me that fishing with Dan was a good idea, Skeeter," she said. "I know how badly you want to catch a tarpon on a fly. Maybe this will get it out of your system."

I doubted that, but wasn't about to say so.

"I don't have to go to work until three on Wednesday," Mom went on, "and I plan to sleep in. I told your father that, so he knows he's in charge."

"Okay," I said, although I knew Mac would be busy with his clients.

The waitress came over then and asked if we were ready for seconds.

"Goodness, no!" said Mom.

"It's all you can eat," the waitress explained patiently.

"Well, I know," said Mom. "But that's all I can eat."

"Me, too," I said. "I'm stuffed."

"I'll pop right out of these jeans if I have one little bitty mouthful more," declared Memaw.

The waitress shook her head, looking real perplexed. Apparently this didn't happen very often. "You sure now?" she asked anxiously. "How about dessert? We got key lime pie, pecan pie, black-bottom pie, cheese cake—"

"Lord have mercy!" Memaw groaned, holding her stomach. "Stop!"

"Just the check, I think, please," said Mom.

As we walked out to the parking lot to get into the car, a black pickup pulled in and squealed to a stop. The truck had big tires that raised it way up off the ground, and it was black with red and yellow flames painted on the sides. There was a sign in the rear window saying THIS TRUCK PROTECTED BY

SMITH & WESSON, and a rifle hung in a gun rack behind the front seat.

The driver got out. His hair was pulled back in a long, blond ponytail. He was big and strong-looking, and his tight sleeveless T-shirt showed every one of the muscles, bulgy veins, and tattoos that lined his arms. I couldn't help staring and thinking, *Now,* this *guy looks like a manatee killer, if I ever saw one*. He had "bad guy" written all over him.

He took off his mirrored sunglasses and stared right back at me as we passed each other. I turned away to see Memaw glaring at the guy with a squint-eyed, just-what-do-you-think-you're-looking-at expression.

Mom said nervously, "Come on, you two."

In the car, Memaw said, "You don't know him, do you, Skeeter?"

I shook my head. But he *had* looked oddly familiar. It took me a minute to realize he looked a little like the manatee killer from my dream the night before. My dream killer had also been one of those tattooed guys who go around acting tough all the time. But looking or acting like a macho dude didn't make a person a manatee killer, at least not in real life. I had to think more scientifically than that.

I remembered something I'd seen on a cop show on TV. When it came to solving a crime, the police used a formula called MOM. It stood for Means, Opportunity, and Motive. The criminal had to have all three.

Did Macho Man have the means to be the killer? Obviously: Smith & Wesson.

Did he have the opportunity? Anybody could rent a boat; people around here did it every day.

That left motive. Which was where I—and everyone else—got stumped. Why in the world would anyone want to shoot a manatee?

Six

When I pulled into Larry's parking lot on my bike, Blink was throwing a ball for Blinky. This was another activity Blink never seemed to tire of. He always had a tennis ball in his pocket, along with our flipping quarter, and he and Blinky played throw and fetch for hours every day.

"Hey, Skeet!" Blink called. He was already reaching into his pocket, an expression of eager anticipation on his face. "Wanna flip?"

"Sure," I answered. I took the quarter from his outstretched hand and we began the game. Blinky stood by with the ball in his mouth, waiting, his crooked tail wagging patiently.

We finished, and Blink put the quarter away. "I'll save it for another day, Skeet."

"That's right, Blink. Save it for another day. Well, I guess I'll go see if Larry needs any bait."

"Okay, Skeet. See ya, Skeet."

"Bye, Blink."

I started to walk away, but Blink called, "You're going fishing with Dirty Dan. Dirty Dan said you're going fishing with him, Skeet."

"Yeah," I said. "I'm going to try for a tarpon on a fly rod."

"You're a lucky duck, Skeet." He grinned.

"I know," I said.

"Lucky duck," he repeated. *"Lucky duck."*

"I sure am," I said.

"Lucky duck," Blink said again.

"Yep."

Blink saying I was lucky was starting to make me feel bad. Dan took Blink—and, of course, Blinky—bait fishing for reds and snappers all the time. But Dan never took Blink fly-fishing for tarpon and, I suddenly realized, he probably never would. Tarpon fishing was too complicated and difficult. Blink could never learn how to do it. Heck, I wasn't sure *I'd* ever learn.

Did Blink wish he was the one going? Or was *lucky duck* one of those phrases he latched on to and liked to repeat? It wasn't easy to figure out what was going on in Blink's head.

For instance, he was real smart about some things. He could name every baseball player on every team, and he could remember all their stats once he heard them. But about a year ago Dan put him in the bathtub with the water running, and didn't think to tell Blink to turn the water *off* when the tub got full. When the camper began to flood, Dan ran into the bathroom to find Blink sitting happily in the overflowing tub, playing with some plastic ships.

I shook my head and went inside the shop to ask Larry if he'd pay me to catch some bait for his tanks. He said he reckoned he could sell some live pinfish if I could get them. He gave me a few pieces of fish scraps, and I headed out in my skiff.

After an hour and a half, I'd filled the minnow bucket with a couple dozen pinfish, and I took them back to the marina quick, before any of them died. Larry counted them, dumped them in the bait tank, and gave me three dollars. That brought my total savings up to thirty-seven dollars. The radio antenna I wanted cost $44.95, so I was getting close.

It was only a little after three o'clock, so I decided to go back out, maybe do a little fishing. The tourist boats tended to stay close to the marina area, where the restaurants and bars were, so I headed downriver, hoping to find a group of snappers I'd have to myself. The water was quiet, though, and I didn't see any signs of fish feeding on the surface. I kept going, and soon I was close to the place where I'd found the manatee. I didn't know why I was doing it really, but I pulled the skiff up to the island to look around.

Some gulls took off, screeching their disapproval at my invasion of their turf. Nothing else moved, except for the river, and the clouds, and the mangrove leaves waving in the wind. The marks Earl and I had seen in the mud the day before had been washed away by the tide. There was nothing to show that anything at all unusual had happened there.

What did I expect to see anyway? The tattooed guy from Fat Boy's parking lot, returning to the scene of the crime? I laughed at the idea.

My eye caught on some trash that had gotten

stuck in the saw grass growing near the high-tide line. All kinds of stuff ended up in the river, and it tended to get bunched up by the movement of the wind and tide. There was an empty gallon milk jug, a Dr Pepper can, a tennis ball, a motor oil bottle, a kid's bright pink flip-flop, a sandwich bag, and a tangle of fishing line.

Junk like that was a fairly common sight, and I hadn't paid any attention to it the day before. Now, for some reason, looking at it made me think of what we were doing in art class in school. Mrs. Rathbun had been talking about still-life painting. She'd told us that when we came back from spring break, we were each supposed to bring in a collection of objects. It wasn't really *homework*, which was why I hadn't mentioned it to Mom. In class, we were going to arrange our objects and draw or paint them.

I figured this was an interesting assortment of things, so I maneuvered the boat to where I could grab them and put them in the minnow bucket. A lot of the stuff was plastic, I realized, but there were plenty of different textures and colors. I was pretty happy with my haul. I even had a title for my picture: *Study in Trash* by Skeet Waters.

On the way home, I stopped at the sheriff's office to check in with Earl.

"Deputy Wells is out on a call," said the woman at the desk. "May I take a message?"

"No," I said. "No message."

As I biked home, I told myself the afternoon wasn't a total waste. I'd made three dollars and picked up some real artistic garbage.

Seven

I didn't want to wish my vacation away, but I could hardly wait to go fishing with Dan. I hung out with Lenny at his house on Monday. He wanted to know what I'd been doing in the sheriff's boat, and I told him about the manatee.

"Cool!" he said. "You're in on an official police investigation."

I explained that I was the only one doing any investigating. "You want to help me look for the body?" I asked.

Lenny nodded eagerly, then frowned. "I forgot for a second. We're leaving tomorrow for Tampa to visit my grandparents. I'll be gone the rest of the vacation."

"Oh," I said, disappointed.

"Mom made me do my English assignment."

"What did you write about?" I asked.

Lenny grinned. "How my pet peeve is writing papers over vacation."

"You did it!" I said. "Let me see."

When I'd finished reading, I told him, "It's good. Funny." I made a face and added, "And very *passionate*."

"Well, I sure hope Mr. G. agrees with you," he said.

With Lenny gone, I spent most of the next day practicing my fly casting in the side yard and waiting to go to Mac's house that night. The time went by really slowly.

Mom didn't get home from work until six-thirty, so dinner was late. I gulped mine down in a few minutes, but it took Mom and Memaw forever to eat. I felt like saying, *Stop talking and chew faster!* I knew better than to ask to be excused early, though. It was my night to do dishes.

Finally, I put my rod in the holder Mac had rigged up on the back of my bike, and fastened my tackle box onto the rack with a bungee cord. When I pulled into Mac's driveway, Dan's and

Earl's trucks were both already there. I went inside, and they all greeted me from the card table, where they were in the middle of a hand.

"Grab yourself a drink from the fridge," Mac offered.

"Give me a minute to take some more money from these fellas, Skeet," said Dan. "Then you and I'll get down to business."

I pulled a chair over to the table to watch. Eager as I was to talk tarpon with Dirty Dan, I always enjoyed sitting in on Mac's poker games. I liked to look at everybody's hands, and listen to them bluff and bet.

As usual, Mac and Earl were drinking beer and munching on chips and peanuts. Dan never ate anything, as far as I could tell, and he never drank anything but Jack Daniel's whiskey. He called it his "butterfly milk."

"Look at this, Skeet," said Mac, holding his cards so I could see them. He had five hearts, a Jack-high flush. It was a pretty good hand, but I knew better than to say so.

"Mmmm," I said.

Mac laughed and said proudly, "That's the way, Skeet." To the other guys he said, "Did you ever see such a poker face? I tell you, when this kid takes up the game, he's gonna beat the pants off all of us."

I tried to keep my poker face, but I couldn't help grinning.

Mac's was a good hand but, as it turned out, not good enough to beat Dirty Dan's full house.

"Time for me to quit and give you boys a fighting chance," said Dan, raking in the pot and pocketing the money. "Skeet and I have work to do."

We sat on the couch on the other side of the room. Dan set his glass and the bottle of Jack Daniel's on the table. Then he put on some powerful-looking reading glasses and said, "Let me see that rod."

I handed him my fly rod and he looked it over intently. While he was examining the reel, I watched him. Dirty Dan was a pretty interesting guy to look at. He wasn't big, but he was strong. Somehow you knew you didn't want to mess with him. His nose had been broken a bunch of times, so it was squashed flat at the top and bent crooked near the end.

The main thing you couldn't help noticing was a ragged, six-inch-long, one-inch-wide scar down the whole left side of his face. The rest of the skin on his face was a deep, leathery brown from all the days he'd spent out in the sun chasing tarpon, but the scarred skin was kind of pinkish brown, tight, and raw-looking.

When I was a little kid, that scar had half fascinated me and half scared me to death. It still fascinated me. Whenever I looked at it now, I thought about the time I'd asked Dan how he got it. I was maybe six or seven years old, and Dan had come over to our house to show Mac how to tie a new kind of tarpon fly. I was hanging around watching and listening, but mostly keeping an eye on that scar. I liked to watch it jump and wiggle around when Dan talked. When there was quiet for a minute, I pointed to his face and said, "What happened?"

"Got my nose broke," said Dan. "Back in my misspent youth."

I didn't know what *that* meant but, anyway, it wasn't what I wanted to know. "I mean *here*," I said, reaching out to point at but not quite touch the scar.

Dan took a long sip of butterfly milk, looked at me with his bloodshot eyes, lifted one eyebrow, and said in a low, slow voice, "Hatchet fight over a blonde." Then he went back to tying his fly.

I remember sitting there, my mind filled with pictures of Dirty Dan fighting with a pirate-y looking guy wearing an eye patch. The pirate-y guy had a hatchet, but that didn't stop Dan. He went after the guy with nothing but his bare hands. While Dan bravely fought, the blond-haired lady cried and begged them to *please stop*.

I sure wished I'd asked Dan more questions then. You can blurt out dumb, rude questions when you're a little kid, and people think it's funny, or at least they don't hold it against you. I was determined to ask for the whole story someday, but the right moment never seemed to come along. It wasn't the kind of thing that came up in normal everyday conversation, in which I might say casually, "Speaking of hatchet fights, Dan, tell me about the one you had over that blonde."

Maybe tomorrow, when Dan and I were out in the boat fishing and talking man to man, I'd have my chance.

Dirty Dan interrupted my thoughts by saying, "We're going to have to take this thing apart."

He was talking about my reel. "How come?" I asked.

He handed me the end of the line and said, "Pull."

I pulled.

"Feel that?" he asked.

"What?"

"There's a little hitch in your drag. Could be some rust in there, or a grain of sand. Anyway, it's no good." He took a drink of butterfly milk. "Come on, let's get this line off here first. You'll want to put on a new one."

As we unspooled the line, Dan said, "When you go after tarpon, there's a hundred things working against you, Skeet. Most of 'em you got no control over. You've got to pay attention to the things you *can* control, and your equipment's one of 'em."

I watched Dan take the reel apart, clean it, oil it, and reassemble it. Then we put on a new fly line. He began tying a nail knot to fasten a length of monofilament line called a leader to the end of my fly line. As I watched Dan's thick, rough fingers at work, he asked, "You know this knot, Skeet?"

"I've tried it," I said, "but I can never get it right."

"It's a tricky devil," Dan agreed. "But you need to know it, and the Bimini twist, the surgeon's loop, and the Huffnagle, too, if you're serious about fishing for tarpon."

I nodded. I was serious, all right. To me, everything about tarpon fishing was incredibly cool. I made a silent vow to get my knot book out and do some practicing at home.

"Now," Dan said as he worked, "if we tied a regular square knot here, what would happen if you put force on it?"

I thought for a minute. "Well, it wouldn't be smooth like a nail knot, so it would get caught in the eyes on the rod."

"Exactly," said Dan. Then he tied on a series of different-strength lines, using the other knots he'd mentioned. "Why am I bothering to do all this?" he asked.

"That first section of line is pretty strong," I said. "What is it, eighty-pound test?"

Dan nodded.

"Well, the next section is only twenty-pound test. If you used a square knot to tie eighty-pound test line to twenty-pound test, the stronger line would wear on the weaker one, and the weak line would eventually break. Probably when you had a fish on."

"You got it," Dan said. "When you're after tarpon, you gotta count on Murphy's Law being in effect. You know Murphy's Law?"

"If anything can go wrong, it will?" I said uncertainly.

"Bingo. Don't forget it."

Dan held up the finished leader and examined it critically. It looked perfect. Each knot was neat, smooth, and strong-looking.

I whistled in admiration.

"You think I tie a good knot, you should have seen my second wife," said Dan. "Her nail knots were beauteous to behold, Skeet. I do miss that woman's knots." He sighed, then muttered, "Too bad she was such a pain in the shorts every otherwise."

That's another thing I liked about Dirty Dan. How many grownups say what they really mean when they're talking to kids?

Suddenly I felt anxious. "Are you sure that twenty-pound section is strong enough?"

"If it's any thicker, he'll see it and he ain't gonna

eat the fly. First order of business is to get him to eat. *Then* we'll worry about how you fight him."

"How do I get him to eat?" I said.

"A perfectly placed cast," he answered.

Uh-oh, I thought. I began wishing I'd spent more time practicing my casting.

"And *this*." He grinned, making the scar wriggle like a snake, and held up a fly. "My secret weapon."

It was a cockroach, which was a fairly common tarpon fly. But I'd never seen one that color. "They like orange?" I asked dubiously.

He lifted an eyebrow and whispered, "They're crazy for it. Like alligators after a poodle. You'll see."

I nodded eagerly.

"*If* you're lucky," he added. "And if you don't make mistakes." He tested each of the knots with a final sharp tug, and nodded with satisfaction. "Looks like you're ready, Skeet," he said.

"What time should I be at the dock?" I asked.

"Six."

"What should I bring?"

"I'll keep your stuff, so just bring yourself. I got everything else we'll need."

"Okay. Thanks, Dan."

"No problemo, Skeet." He poured himself a fresh glass of butterfly milk. "Here's to luck," he said, and took a long slug.

"Sounds like I'm going to need it."

"You're going to need some sleep, too," said Dan.

That got Mac's attention and he looked at his watch. "Oops, how'd it get so late? Skeet, you'd better get on home now or your mama'll skin me alive and feed me to the sharks."

I went over to give Mac a hug and say good night to the other guys.

"Sleep tight, Skeeter," said Earl.

"Okay," I said. But I didn't think there was much chance of *that*.

Eight

I ate a quick breakfast and got to the dock at ten minutes to six the next morning. Dirty Dan was already in his boat arranging my rod in the side compartment, where it would be safe once we got moving. Dan had a boat that was specially made for fishing on the flats, the big areas of shallow water where tarpon often feed. It was much smaller than Mac's boat, or even my skiff, and could run in only six inches of water. On its side were the words *Tarpon Man*.

"Push us off and let's go, Skeet," he said without taking his eyes off what he was doing. "We got ourselves a bluebird day."

I looked at the sky. It was still dark, with only

the faintest sign of light in the east, and I could see the glitter of stars. When you're hunting for tarpon in the shallows, you need to be able to see them. You want a bright, clear sky with no clouds, and that was what we had, or would have when the sun got higher.

"Great," I said. I unhooked the bow and stern lines from the cleats on the dock and hopped into the boat.

Dan cranked up the engine, and we motored slowly through the restricted part of the river, sending herons, egrets, and cormorants into lazy flight. Mac and most of the other guides were just meeting their clients at the marina or having a last cup of coffee at Betty's Diner, so we were the first boat to head out.

I loved the river at this time of morning, when it was quiet and peaceful, with a haze of fog hanging over it. I could hardly believe that the day I'd thought so much about was actually happening.

When we left the refuge area of the river, Dan opened it up and we sped through the curves and zigzags. We were hauling! The boat itself wasn't much, but Dan's engine was huge.

He hollered over the noise, "There's a big silver king out here with your name on it, Skeet."

I was already smiling from the speed and excitement, but I could feel my grin grow wider at that.

We came to the mouth of the river and ran out in the gulf for about forty-five minutes. Then Dan pulled up to a long, deserted stretch of shoreline and cut the engine. He picked up his push pole and jumped up onto the platform above the motor. He was quick for a guy Memaw's age. Immediately, he began to use the pole to move the boat slowly and quietly across the shallow water, his eyes scanning the surface intently.

"Now hand me my butterfly milk, Skeet, and let's catch you a tarpon."

I was surprised, not only because it seemed a little early for a drink but also because Mac never drank when he had a client in his boat. Some guides did, but Mac said it was asking for trouble. I wasn't a client, though. I opened the cooler, thinking I'd get a glimpse of what Dan had brought for our lunch. There was nothing inside except the bottle of Jack Daniel's, a moldy hunk of cheese in a Baggie, some chewed-up tarpon flies, and a near-empty jar of mustard.

I handed Dirty Dan the bottle and asked, "Where's the rest of the stuff, up in the storage compartment?"

But Dan didn't seem to hear me, he was so focused on the water. I got my rod and stood up in my place on the bow. I looked back at Dan and said, "This is so great! I sure wish I could pay you."

"You catch a tarpon, Skeet, that'll be pay enough." He took a drink from the bottle, set it down between his feet, and kept poling. "Okay, now, till the sun gets higher, we're looking for rollers," he said. "You see any, tell me where and which direction they're heading in, and I'll try to get you in a position to cast."

I'd read as much as I could about tarpon, and asked Mac about a million questions over the years, so I knew about rollers. Tarpon are weird in the fish world, because they come up sometimes to breathe. When they break the surface to grab a gulp of air, it's called rolling. You can see their backs then, or maybe a glimpse of a dorsal fin, and you can also tell which way they're swimming.

Spotting rollers sounds easier than it is. They're up for only a second, and it takes a lot of experience to be able to tell which direction they're heading in—experience that I didn't have.

I never saw anything, even though I was looking hard. But a minute later Dan said, "There." He began poling faster but just as sneakily toward whatever he had seen. "Oh, they're high and happy, exactly the way we want 'em, Skeet."

I squinted my eyes, but didn't see anything.

"Okay, get ready. There's fish coming. See that nervous water?"

When fish are moving, the water above them looks different, sort of quivery, or "nervous." I've seen it sometimes when Mac's pointed it out to me, times when the water was dead calm and glassy. But today there was enough of a breeze to give the entire surface a ripple, and all the water looked quivery.

I nodded, but the truth was, I didn't see what he was talking about. As far as I could tell, the only thing that was nervous was *me*.

"They're coming left to right at two o'clock, about a hundred twenty feet. You see 'em?"

My heart was pounding like crazy. Dan's directions were perfectly clear, or should have been. I knew that if the boat was a clock face, the bow where I stood was twelve o'clock. But I was so anxious that I had to stop and picture a clock, and think about whether two o'clock was to my left or my right. Right. Okay. But forget about calculating a hundred twenty feet. Instead, I turned to see where Dan was looking.

"Okay, okay, they're at a hundred feet. You ready?" asked Dan.

"Yeah." I started to lift my rod to cast.

"No! Not yet! Wait till they're closer. You see 'em?"

"No," I admitted desperately.

"One o'clock now, eighty feet out. Okay, get ready. Ready? Go ahead and cast—now!"

I did, but my timing was way off. Instead of landing softly and enticingly in the fish's path, the fly landed with an ugly splat right on top of them. They spooked and took off, leaving only a muddy swirl where they had been. Casting to a real fish sure was different from casting to a pop can in the yard.

Dan took a sip from the bottle.

"Sorry," I muttered miserably.

"No sweat, Skeet," he said calmly. "You'll get

the next one. The important thing is learning from your mistakes. Do you know what you did wrong?"

"Everything," I said.

Dan didn't disagree. He just asked, "What was the main thing?"

I thought for a minute. "I never really saw the fish before I made the cast," I admitted.

Dan nodded. "You'll get better at spotting 'em as the day goes on," he said. "For right now, you don't *have* to see 'em as long as you put the fly where I tell you. Now, what kept you from doing that?"

"Jitters, mostly, I guess."

"It happens. You'll settle down." Dan was more confident of my improvement than I was. "Take another cast," he directed. "Forty feet, nine o'clock."

I did my best.

"Sixty feet, eleven o'clock."

We did this for a while. After every cast, Dan helped me figure out what I had done wrong. I was concentrating like crazy, and he was watching me real closely and analyzing every move I made.

Then he took the rod. "See that gob of seaweed floating over there?" he asked.

"Yeah."

"I'm going to cast toward it. Watch how the line lays out on the water."

He made a beautiful, smooth cast. The fly and all the line landed lightly and delicately on the surface at the same time.

"Wow," I said. "That was *perfect.*"

"Now, this time, watch my back cast. To get that nice, soft landing you gotta keep your loop tight on the back cast and time your forward cast just right."

"Wow," I said again, after he'd demonstrated. "That was amazing." What else was there to say? Dirty Dan wasn't known as the Tarpon Man for nothing. If he'd been casting to a fish, there was no way he wouldn't have caught it.

He handed the rod back. "Okay, you try."

I made some more casts. They were all embarrassing, but Dan managed to find something encouraging to say after each one. I could feel myself beginning to relax a little.

The sun was pretty high in the sky by then, and Dan said, "Okay, Skeet. You got your jitters out. The visibility's good. We're going to move to another spot."

"Okay," I said. "Where are we going?"

"You'll see," he said, taking a drink from the bottle and setting it between his legs as he sat at the wheel. "I thought about blindfolding you, but I figure I can trust you, seeing as you're Mac's kid."

I nodded eagerly.

"Of course, you understand that if you ever tell anybody about this spot, I'll have to kill you."

I laughed, then looked at Dan's face. I thought I saw a smile tickle the corners of his mouth, but I wasn't sure. I laughed again, a little nervously this time. "Don't worry. My lips are sealed," I said.

He nodded approvingly. "That's the way, Skeet. Some things just oughtta stay secret."

Nine

As Dan began slowly poling the boat, I saw what made this location so special. The water was four to six feet deep, with large stretches of light-colored, sandy bottom and hardly any grass.

"The sun's nice and high now," said Dan. "What you gotta remember is that the water can be a mirror or a window. Look *at* it and all you'll see is a reflection of the sky. Look *through* it and you'll see what's below the surface."

I practiced looking through the water. But when Dan said in a low, urgent voice, "Fish at ten o'clock, Skeet. Coming right toward us," I didn't see a thing.

I looked toward ten o'clock and got my rod ready anyway.

"Don't cast yet, he's still too far. See him? Two hundred feet."

"No," I said, squinting in frustration, willing my eyes to see something.

"Oh, boy, there's three of 'em. See 'em now?"

I shook my head.

"Those glasses polarized?" Dan asked.

I nodded. Without polarized lenses, there was no hope of seeing the fish, sun or no sun.

"You looking through the water, not at it?"

"Yeah."

I peered and scrunched my eyes tighter, but I couldn't for the life of me see what Dan saw. Then, all at once, I did! Three dark shapes moving over the light sandy bottom. "I see 'em!" I shouted. "Coming this way!"

"Okay, now," said Dan very calmly. "Settle down, get ready, and think about your cast. You want to put it about three yards in front of 'em, nice and easy."

I made my cast, but it was too far to the right. The fish kept swimming, paying no attention to my fly, and finally spooked when they saw the boat. I muttered in disgust.

But Dan only said, "The thing about a tarpon, Skeet, is that he's lazier than an old dog in the noonday sun. Lots of the time, he won't move five inches out of his way, even for a meal. You gotta put it right where he almost *has* to eat it, or else smack into it. And sometimes even that isn't good enough."

He took another sip of butterfly milk and grinned. "It wouldn't be any fun if it was easy, now, would it?"

To be honest, I could have gone for a little easy fun right about then, but I wasn't going to admit it to Dan.

On my next cast, the lead fish in a group of four turned toward my fly. "Eat it, eat it, eat it!" Dan urged.

When the fish turned away and kept on swimming, I moaned. "Aww, man, what do you want?"

"Leave it, leave it!" Dan told me. "The next one might take it."

But the next one didn't, and neither did the two after that. "Aww, man!" I cried again.

Dan seemed happy, though. "That was real good, Skeet. You almost got 'em to eat."

Maybe it was all the talk of eating, but suddenly I was starving. Thirsty, too. I looked at my watch. It was ten-thirty. We'd been out for four and a half hours and Dan hadn't sat down once, so neither had I. He'd been sipping from the whiskey bottle, but I hadn't had anything. My legs felt a little wobbly.

"I'm just gonna grab a drink," I said, laying my rod carefully on the bow. "Where do you keep them?"

"Cooler," he said, but his attention was on the water, not the question.

I'd already looked in the cooler, but I stepped down to look again. Could I have missed seeing a six-pack of soda and a sack of sandwiches? My foot landed on a coil of frayed blue nylon rope lying on the bottom of the boat, and I slipped on it and almost fell. Mac kept his boat shipshape, and had taught me to do the same, but I'd noticed Dan didn't seem to care so much about neatness.

"I guess you could stow that," he said absent-mindedly, his attention, as always, on the water.

When I looked in the front storage compartment to find a place for the rope, I saw a handgun lying in a molded-plastic gun case. Either the case had been left open or it had jiggled open from the movement of the boat. I wasn't too surprised to see it since where we live lots of people have guns. Pickup trucks like the one we'd seen at Fat Boy's, with a gun rack behind the driver's seat, were a common sight.

It drove Mom crazy. Mac had had a gun for a while, but she'd made him get rid of it. I knew Larry kept one behind the counter at the marina. Of course Earl had one, being a deputy.

Dan must have noticed me looking at it because he said, "Next hammerhead tries to steal a fish of mine gets shot between the eyes. I'm too old to be out in the water wrestling sharks."

I grinned the way I did every time I pictured Dan bonking that hammerhead on the noggin with his club. "Aww, but shootin' 'em doesn't make half as good a story," I answered.

That made me think of the story of how Dan got his scar, in the hatchet fight over the blond-haired lady. Maybe Dan would tell me the whole thing while we had lunch. I put the line away and opened the cooler again to look for something to drink. There was the same hunk of cheese, which I now saw had been nibbled on, and the empty mustard jar. There hadn't been any food or sodas in the storage compartment, either. With a sinking feeling, I realized that Dan hadn't brought lunch, and neither had I.

"Just bring yourself," he'd told me, and, stupidly, that's what I'd done. Dan had said he had everything we'd need, and I guessed from his point of view we *did*. We had fishing gear—and a bottle of Jack Daniel's.

Mac always kept some cans of soda, some munchies, and a big jug of fresh water in his boat, and so did I. It was another of Mom's rules, for "just in case." If she had been up when I left the house, she would have asked a million questions: Do you have your lunch? Your drinks? Your hat? There are life jackets in the boat, right?

But she had left all this to Mac, saying he was in charge. And Mac wasn't used to worrying about whether or not I had lunch. It was the kind of thing that had been happening ever since Mac moved down the street. Some things fell through the cracks.

As for me, I'd been so jacked up about this trip, I hadn't thought about anything but tarpon. I gulped, and my throat was so dry I could hardly swallow.

I took another look in the storage compartment. There *was* a plastic milk jug half hidden underneath a wadded-up rain slicker, next to an open bag holding paper cups.

"Is this fresh water?" I asked.

"Fresh enough," Dan replied.

I poured some into a cup and took a big swallow. Warm. Hot, almost. Yuck. I dumped out the rest and screwed the cap back on the jug.

For the next two hours, I tried not to think about how thirsty I was as Dan continued to pole us over the flats. I felt kind of swimmy-headed, and the sun off the water was lulling me into a daze. I couldn't understand how he did it, but Dan seemed as alert as ever. There was no way I was going to punk out first when he was the one who was doing the hard work.

By two o'clock, I estimated I'd made a million casts and done a million things wrong. I'd stepped on my own line, gotten it caught in my belt buckle, worked it into some spectacular tangles, cast too far, not far enough, and in the wrong direction. I'd stuck the hook of the fly in my own back, and, once, would have taken Dan's eye out if he hadn't been wearing sunglasses. I figured I'd spooked every fish in the entire Gulf of Mexico.

Through it all, Dan never got mad or impatient, and he didn't yell at me once. He actually managed to act as if he believed every cast was going to be *the one*, long after I'd secretly given up hope.

I ate the piece of cheese, figuring it was probably Blink who had nibbled on it. I was so hungry it actually tasted okay. By then, that sun-warmed water was going down pretty good, too. Whenever I took a sip, I pretended it was Memaw's homemade lemonade sliding down my sandpapery throat, cool and wet and sour-sweet.

"Fish! Eleven o'clock!"

Dirty Dan's shout startled me out of my daze, and I just about fell overboard. I shook my head to clear it. I couldn't see anything but the sun's reflection on the water, and I forced myself to concentrate and peer through the wicked glare on the surface. After a couple of seconds I saw the long, dark shape coming closer. Coming fast. I was going to have to make a short cast, but a tricky one.

"Take it easy, Skeet," Dan said, almost in a whisper. "Just drop it in front of him, real gentle."

Maybe because I didn't have too much time to think about it, that's what I did.

"Good, good, now strip your line in, strip, strip . . ." Dan was saying to me in a low voice. Then, to the fish, "Eat it, eat it, come on, eat it . . ."

And the fish ate! He took my fly!

"Okay, keep stripping. He's gonna feel it in a minute," Dan said. "Wait till he starts to turn and— *Now! Set the hook!*"

I pulled back hard to make the hook dig in. And two seconds later that tarpon came busting right out of the water, thrashing its whole body in an amazing, acrobatic arch, trying to throw my hook and escape.

"Don't pull back on him now, Skeet!" Dan hollered. "Drop your rod tip—remember, you gotta bow to the king when he jumps. Give him line and let him run. I'm pretty sure he's hooked in the corner of his mouth. It's not coming out."

I "bowed to the king," dipping the end of my rod to give the fish plenty of line while it was fresh and full of crazy fight. I let him run, and when I heard the *zzziiing!* of the line flying off my reel, I shouted, "*Weee-oooow!*"

Dirty Dan was shouting, too. "*Yee-ha, Skeeter! Look at him go!*"

"I guess that lazy old dog's awake now!" I hollered. "And he doesn't seem too happy!"

At the end of his run, the fish came up out of the water again in a dazzling leap of silver, shaking his head, his big mouth wide open.

"He's *humongous*!" I cried.

"He's big, all right!" said Dan, sounding just as excited as I was. "Hundred twenty pounds, hundred thirty, maybe."

"He's a *monster*!"

"Yessir, he's a beauty," Dan agreed. "Okay, now, okay, let's get him in. We ain't got him yet, Skeet."

My heart was racing so fast I had to stop and make myself take a deep breath and try to settle down. I knew Dan was right: hooking him was only half the battle. Now I had to get him to the boat. I'd heard enough fishing stories over the years to know that this was the time when Murphy's Law was most likely to kick in. Apply too much pressure—or not enough pressure—at the wrong time, and the line would break. Leave too much slack, and the line could get wrapped around the fish, or be cut by its sharp gill plates. One of the knots might let go. There was no end to what could go wrong.

But with Dirty Dan the Tarpon Man coaching me, I managed not to do anything seriously stupid. I fought that fish for close to an hour. Time and time again I'd get him close to the boat, thinking he was tired enough to bring in, and he'd make another furious run, taking out all the line I'd gained. My arms ached from lifting and reeling, lifting and reeling, over and over again. I knew if this went on too long, he could chew through the leader and get away.

"I'll let you go, honest," I called to the fish. "Just let me get you in and touch you!"

The fish responded by making another run.

"That run was shorter, Skeet, you see that?" Dan said. "You got him beat now if you don't let up. Keep the pressure on. Don't let him rest."

When do I *get to rest?* I wondered. My arm muscles were burning, but I kept the pressure on.

"Now give him the down and dirty," Dan told me.

I knew all about the down and dirty from all the stories I'd heard over the years about catching tarpon. As soon as a fish showed signs of slowing down, you hit him with the down and dirty, trying to wear him out. I lowered the tip of my rod so it was under water, and pulled back on it strong and steady, turning the fish around. When he started coming the way I'd turned him, I switched back the other way.

"That's it," said Dan. "Keep after him. Anything he wants to do, don't let him. Everything he tries to do, show him he can't. Turn him around till he doesn't know which way is up."

I gave him the down and dirty over and over again. Man, he was one tough fish. I was beginning to think I was no match for him when finally I could feel the fight go out of him. Soon after, I was able to reel the end of my leader through the eye at the tip of my rod, the sign that a fish was officially "caught."

I took a long look at that beautiful creature, trying to memorize everything about it. It was six feet from its head to the tip of its tail! I reached out to touch its big, tough, silvery scales. They were huge, probably four inches across. I'd heard of people pulling one out to keep for a souvenir, but it seemed a sorry thing to do to such a spectacular creature.

"Thanks," I whispered.

It was time to take a photo and release the fish. I hadn't thought to bring a camera, and though I knew Mac always kept one to record his clients' big moments, I wasn't going to ask Dan if he had one. I knew he didn't. It didn't matter. I'd never forget one single thing about this fish, or this day.

I nodded to Dan. He used the pliers to remove the hook, and my fish slipped back into the water and swam away.

I reached over to shake Dan's hand, the way I'd seen clients do when Mac was guiding them, but he grabbed me in a back-slapping embrace. "Good going, Skeet. You fought him like a pro!"

"Thanks, Dan. I'm—it was—" But for the moment, I had no words for the way I felt. I pounded his back in return, tears of exhaustion and awe and pure happiness pooling in my eyes. All my moments of doubt and uncertainty, of hunger, thirst, and discomfort, were forgotten. I had caught my first tarpon on a fly.

Ten

We sat for a while talking about the fish and the fight, reliving every moment for the sheer pleasure of it. At around three-thirty, Dan said we'd better head in. I was putting away my rod when I had a sudden idea. "Hey, Dan! Could we get on the radio to Mac and tell him about my fish?"

Dan took a sip from his bottle. "No radio," he said. "I lost a big tarpon one day when my fly line got tangled on the antenna. I was so mad I ripped the darn thing off." He grinned. "Much better that way."

I shouldn't have been surprised. To Dirty Dan's way of thinking, a radio wasn't a good thing to have in case of an emergency; it was a possible hindrance to landing a fish. That's why he was the Tarpon Man.

"No sweat," I said, thinking I was glad Mom was at work so there was no chance of meeting her at the dock when we got back. If she knew I'd been out all day with no radio, no food, no fresh water, not to mention with a bottle of whiskey and a gun in the boat—well, I didn't even want to think about how mad she'd be, at me and Mac both. No way I wanted to be the cause of another fight. Plus, I'd never be allowed to go fishing with Dirty Dan again, that was for sure.

Thinking of Mom reminded me that I was supposed to wear a life jacket when we were running. Guiltily, I realized I hadn't worn one on the way out. I'd have put one on for the ride home, but—no surprise this time—there weren't any.

I peeked at the bottle of whiskey and saw it was pretty near empty. Uh-oh. Was Dan drunk? He didn't seem to be. I watched him stow his push pole and let the engine down. He moved around the boat quickly and easily, not stumbling or staggering like drunks in the movies. The whiskey didn't seem to have any effect on him. So why not just drink water, I wondered.

Dan asked, "Ready to roll, Skeet?" His voice sounded normal, too, not slurry and mumbly like a drunk's.

I gave a mental shrug and said, "Ready!"

We took off, zooming across the flats, and all my worried thoughts blew away with the breeze. I could hardly believe it: I'd caught a tarpon!

At Larry's, I helped Dan secure the boat. I was thanking him for the thousandth time when Blink walked up. Blinky was by his side, a ball in his mouth.

"Hi, Dirty Dan! Hi, Skeet!" Blink said. Instead of his usual smile, though, Blink wore a worried expression. His eyes blinked even faster than normal, and his gaze flew anxiously from Dirty Dan to me and back to Dan again. He sounded nervous. I noticed he hadn't reached into his pocket for the flipping quarter.

"Hey, Blink," I said, "what's up?"

Dan smiled and gave his son's shoulder a pat. "How's it going, Blink?"

Blink seemed to relax a little at that, but he asked, "Is Dirty Dan mad?"

"Mad?" said Dan. He looked as puzzled as I felt by Blink's question.

"Was Skeet bad? Did Dirty Dan have to get mad?" Blink went on.

An odd expression passed over Dan's face. Then he smiled quickly and said, "Heck, no. Skeet here got himself a tarpon. What do you think of that?"

"Skeet got a tarpon," Blink repeated. "That's good, Skeet." I was glad to see his face split into a huge grin. "Skeet got a tarpon."

"I sure did," I said. "He was a beauty. And, believe me, nobody's mad—except maybe the fish."

Blink got a big kick out of that. He kept laughing and saying over and over, "Skeet caught a beauty and nobody's mad but the fish!"

Then I saw him reach into his pocket. Before he could say it, I did: "Wanna flip?"

Blink found that hilarious, too. He said, "*No*, Skeet, *I* say 'Wanna flip?' Remember? *I* say it. *Then* we play."

"Oh, right," I said. "I forgot. Okay, you say it."

"Wanna flip?"

"Sure."

We played one game, and I was happy to see

he'd forgotten about Dan and me being bad or mad or whatever he'd been so worried about. I said, "Blink, I'll play again, but I've *gotta* get something to drink first."

"And I think I'll go take a shower and sit in the air-conditioning for a while," said Dan.

"Okay, Dan. Hey, thanks," I said as he turned to go. "That was so great. It was the best day of my life. Really, I mean it."

Dan smiled. "You did good, Skeet. Tell Mac I said so. You coming, Blink?"

"Skeet and I are going to play again, Dirty Dan," Blink answered.

"All right. You come on home after, have some supper."

Blink and I went into the marina, followed by Blinky. I didn't have any money with me, but Larry said to take whatever I wanted on credit. Blink announced to the whole store that Skeet caught a tarpon and it was a beauty and nobody was mad but the fish, so after I slugged down a can of soda, then another, I told the story to Larry and Blink and Blinky and two guys who were hanging around. They were as attentive an audience as I could have hoped for, and they had a lot of questions, too. So I opened a third can of soda and a bag of chips and sat down on the old wooden stool by the counter. I finally had a good fish story of my own, and I figured on taking my sweet time telling it.

Eleven

When I got home, Mom wasn't back from work yet. Memaw looked up from the newspaper she was reading, and her blue eyes got real big. "Why, Skeeter," she said, "your face is redder than my good boots!"

I glanced in the mirror and groaned. I'd forgotten sunscreen, along with everything else. The constant, blaring sun was another aspect of Florida living that freaked Mom out. She worried all the time about sunburn and skin cancer. It was a real concern for fishing guides who were out on the water all the time, and another problem Mom had with Mac's way of life.

"Come on in the bathroom with me right now,"

said Memaw. "Let's get something on that before your mother gets home and has a conniption."

Memaw doused me in aloe gel, talking the whole time about an ad she'd seen in the paper for a Chinese restaurant called the Golden Moon, which had just opened in town.

"I've never been to a Chinese restaurant, old as I am. Can you believe it? First chance we get, I want to take you and your mama there. We'll try everything on the menu, even if it sounds peculiar. I hear they do cook some peculiar dishes. But we won't be squeamish, will we, Skeeter? I've never been squeamish a day in my life and I don't intend to start now. I can't abide people who won't try new things, can you? Where's the fun in that?"

Memaw loved trying new things and she loved going out to eat. She always said that any meal she didn't have to cook was a good one.

As soon as I was able to get a word in, I told her about my tarpon, and she got just as excited about that as she'd been about eating Chinese food. Then Mom came home and I told the whole story again, but not until after she had her "conniption" about my sunburn. Memaw's aloe had made the burn feel cooler, but it hadn't done anything to hide the redness.

Mom put more aloe on me, fussing the whole time. "Didn't your father give you sunscreen?" Luckily, I didn't have time to answer before she went on. "And that Dan! You'd think a grown man would act more responsible, especially when he's in charge of someone else's child."

"Mom, you make it sound like I'm a little kid," I protested. "It's not Mac's fault I forgot to use sunscreen, or Dan's either. Besides," I lied, "this sunburn looks a lot worse than it feels." Seeing how upset she was, I hoped more than ever that she'd never know all the parts of the story I'd left out.

By the time we'd eaten dinner and I'd called Mac and told the fish story again, I was beat. It wasn't until I was in bed and about to drift off that I realized I hadn't thought about the manatee all day. I got up and dialed Mac's number again.

"Hey, Mac, I forgot to ask you. Did you talk to Earl today? Did they find out anything about who killed that manatee?"

"I did talk to him, and they haven't learned a thing," Mac answered. "Earl feels bad, 'cause he says they're not really trying. It's like he told you the first day—they're busy, and there's nothing to go on."

The news—or lack of it—was about what I'd expected, but it was still disappointing. "Okay," I said. "I was just wondering."

"Hey, did you get a picture of that tarpon?" Mac asked.

"No camera," I explained. "But that's okay—"

Mac interrupted to say, " 'Cause you've got a picture in your brain, don't you?"

"Yeah," I said.

"And that isn't ever going to fade."

I nodded. Then, remembering we were on the phone, I said, "I can still see it clear as anything."

"I know, buddy," said Mac. "I know."

The cool thing was, he really *did* know.

"Listen, Skeet, I'm leaving tomorrow to trail the boat down to the Keys to meet a client. I'm going to fish him for four or five days, depending on how things go."

"Oh," I said. "Okay. Is it that guy from Chicago who talks on his cell phone the whole time you're out in the boat?"

Mac chuckled. "The very same. He's sure got a

funny idea about 'getting away from it all.' But what the heck. He's okay, and he's a big tipper, if I can find us some fish."

"You will," I said.

"Listen, buddy, you have a good time on the rest of your vacation, and I hope you hear something about that manatee soon."

"Yeah, me, too. Well, have fun, Mac."

"I'll try. And I'll call you when I get back in town."

"Bye."

In bed, as I drifted off, I had a funny thought about parents and kids. Mom tried, but she didn't get why tarpon fishing was so incredibly cool. And Mac tried, but he wasn't the type to make sure I ate lunch, wore sunscreen, went to bed on time, and stuff like that. Maybe that was why parents came in pairs, at least at the beginning, so one could cover the stuff the other didn't.

Now that Mom and Mac weren't together, maybe I was going to have to take care of more things for myself. I kind of wanted to think about that a little, but I must have fallen asleep two seconds later, in spite of my sunburn.

When I woke up the next morning, the dead

manatee was on my mind again, along with my tarpon. I stretched and groaned at the pain in both arms. It was a good kind of pain, though, a badge of honor.

I lay in bed, flexing my arms and thinking. Earl had hypothesized that the manatee's killer towed the dead body behind a boat and cut it loose someplace way out in the Gulf of Mexico. But it was possible, I reasoned, that the manatee hadn't been taken so far out. And depending on the wind direction, it might have washed up on shore far from where I'd found it the first time, but not *too* far. It was possible, also, that the killer had towed it into the tangled maze of the backcountry. Either way, there was a chance that if I went out in my skiff looking, I'd find it. And if I did, we'd have some evidence of a crime, and with *that*, maybe somebody would actually work on finding the killer.

A little voice kept telling me it wasn't likely that I'd find the body, but I'd felt the same way about the odds of my catching a tarpon, and look what happened. Anyway, I thought, I was on vacation and had the time.

I told myself I could work on my English paper.

But then I remembered I only had to write a first draft. No big deal.

I didn't need much convincing to go cruising around in my boat. I grinned, thinking, *And this time I'll take plenty of food, sodas, and fresh water, and put on a ton of sunscreen.* I needed another eight dollars before I could get a radio antenna, but it was a clear, calm, sunny day, and I wasn't worried about the weather.

As it turned out, Mom said I could go, but she insisted on putting sunscreen on me herself this time. I tried not to flinch as she touched my reddened skin. She also gave me an extremely stupid-looking hat with a big brim and earflaps, and made me promise to wear it. I didn't argue, though, because at least she was letting me go. Greasy with sunscreen from head to toe, smelling like a giant coconut, and looking just as ridiculous, I finally got out of the house.

I took off the hat as soon as I was out of sight. Then, steering the skiff downriver, I knew I had to make a decision. Was I going to look for the manatee's body floating out in the gulf or washed up onshore? The idea of trying to find something in miles of open ocean was discouraging, so I decided to search the channels that crisscrossed among the saw grass and mangrove keys closer to shore. The tide was almost high, so the water was deep enough for my skiff, and I'd have several hours before it dropped too low to run the boat in the backcountry.

I began at "the scene of the crime," which was how I'd been thinking of the place where I'd found the manatee. Then I took the first channel that branched off the main river. I kept my speed slow so I could scan the edges of the mangroves for anything out of the ordinary, the ordinary being mangrove roots and the small fish and crabs that sheltered beneath them, and the occasional buoy or piece of trash left behind by humans.

I worked systematically, following the meandering path of each channel to its end, then turning back to the river and going to the next channel and starting over. It was fun actually, and I was having a good time exploring all the secret, hidden places most people never saw. I spotted snook and redfish and little snappers in the shallow water, and lots of birds, and found a few new fishing spots I'd never have discovered otherwise. Once, I spotted a large, dark mass in the mangrove roots and got excited, but it turned out to be a plastic garbage bag.

The tide became too low for my boat to navigate the backcountry waters, so I headed for home. I felt frustrated, and began to think maybe the police were right not to be spending their time on this.

When I reached the house, Memaw was waiting for me. "Skeeter, your mama has to work late tonight, and she said for us to go ahead and eat without her. I'm thinking we ought to go to that new Chinese restaurant for supper. We can bring some back for her. What do you say?"

"Sure," I answered. "Just let me take a quick shower first."

On the way to the restaurant, Memaw talked a mile a minute. "Now, Skeet, don't be surprised if we're supposed to take off our shoes and sit on the floor to eat. I heard that in China people do that. Or maybe that's in Japan . . . I wore pants and these sandals slip right off, so I'm ready for anything. I know I said I'd sample whatever's on the menu, but I've been thinking about it, and I don't believe I can eat a thing that's still alive. I don't relish the idea of my food fighting back when I stick my fork in it, do you? Although I suppose we'll be using chopsticks. I hadn't thought of that. Well, I'll try anything else—eel, octopus, that soup they make with bird nests, even though I heard it has bird saliva in it, can you imagine?—as long as it's not squirming." She paused for a second and asked, "Do you think your gramma's a terrible ninny, Skeeter?"

I told Memaw that I liked my food to be dead, too, definitely not alive or even wounded, and said I didn't think that meant we were ninnies.

At the Golden Moon, no one asked for our shoes and we were seated at a regular table instead of on the floor, and I thought Memaw looked a tiny bit disappointed. But she perked right up when we were handed our menus.

Memaw read the first line aloud: " 'WELCOME TO THE GOLDEN MOON. YOU ARE THE CUSTOMER. THE CUSTOMER IS BOOS.' " She looked at me, a puzzled expression on her face. We both started laughing at the same moment, realizing that someone had typed "boos" instead of "boss."

Memaw composed herself and said, "Personally, I've always been partial to a restaurant where the customer is boos."

That set me giggling again. But Memaw had

moved on down the menu. “Can you believe these prices, Skeeter? They’re so reasonable,” she exclaimed. “We can afford to get anything you like. Oh, look here! It says you can order a combination plate. You can try lots of different foods, just like we wanted to.”

I scanned the menu to see what she meant. It *was* pretty cool. There were four columns, marked A, B, C, and D. If you ordered a combination platter, you could choose one dish from each column.

“Let’s do that, Skeeter!” Memaw said excitedly.

“Yeah,” I said. “That way, we’ll be able to try eight different things, if we share.”

“I’m just going to close my eyes and point and see what I get.”

“I think I’m going to be more scientific,” I said. “I’m going to make sure no two things I order have any of the same words in them. That way, I’ll be sure to get a good variety, right?”

“That’s just brilliant, Skeeter!” Memaw said, beaming.

When we’d both decided what we wanted, I looked over the remaining pages of the menu. Pointing to a dish called Happy Family, I said, “That was us until Mom threw Mac out.”

Memaw sighed. "I don't know what your mama's doing. I'm not sure she does. Right now she thinks being apart from your daddy is going to make her happy. But I'm afraid your mama has never had much of a talent for happiness. It's something I don't understand."

I thought about that. It was true that Mom always seemed to be thinking about what was wrong, or how things could be better. It was as if she couldn't see what was good about our lives. She seemed to think everything that wasn't perfect was Mac's fault.

"What's going to happen?" I was afraid to hear the answer, even as I asked the question.

"We'll have to wait and see, Skeeter. I know it's hard."

We were quiet for a while. Then Memaw pointed to something on the menu called Ten Thousand Delights. "Tell you what," she said, smiling at me with a hint of mischief in her eyes. "Let's order your mama this."

That was one thing I really loved about Memaw: it was impossible for her to stay gloomy for long. I smiled back and said, "Maybe it'll cheer her up. It's worth a try."

The waitress came then to take our orders, and I checked her out. She looked Chinese, but she was wearing an ordinary white shirt and black pants, and I realized I'd expected some sort of costume, like the ones I'd seen in *National Geographic* magazine. After Memaw placed her order, she asked, "Nothing in there will be squirming, will it?"

The waitress looked puzzled. "Squirming?" I could see that she not only found the word difficult to pronounce but had no idea what it meant.

Memaw said, "You know, *squirming*." She did a little shimmy with her shoulders and wiggled her fingers in the air. "Alive."

The waitress looked distressed.

"Still moving," Memaw explained. To demonstrate further, she stood up, wriggled her hips, and snapped her fingers, making her eyes wide and lively, and smiling like crazy. I have to say, she looked alive, all right.

The waitress, with an expression of alarm on her face, looked at me for help, but I was laughing too hard to say anything. She turned and fled into a back room.

"Where did she go? And what is so funny?" Memaw said with surprise.

Finally, a man came from the back and asked if he could help us. His English was a lot better than the waitress's, and Memaw's fears of wiggly food were put to rest.

When our plates came, we tried gamely to eat with the chopsticks we were given, but we were both pretty hopeless. The waitress saw us struggling and brought us forks, so we were able to chow down. I didn't know what I was eating half the time, but it was all good—and, as Memaw pointed out, definitely dead.

"That paper you've got to write, Skeeter, what's it about?" she asked.

"A pet peeve." I made a face. "Mr. G.'s idea of a 'fun' assignment."

"Well, it could be worse," Memaw said. "You've actually got something you're really peeved about."

"What?" I asked. Then, before she answered, I got it. "Oh, you mean the manatee. Yeah. Hey, that's not a bad idea."

Memaw looked pleased with herself. Then she asked me what I'd done all day, so I told her about my fruitless search for the manatee's body. She eyed me shrewdly. "You gonna give up?" she asked.

"Well, it sort of seems like a waste of time," I said.

"You have some other big, important plans? Besides your schoolwork, I mean?"

"No."

"Well," Memaw said, "it's only Thursday. You've still got a three-day weekend ahead."

That was true. And even though I hadn't found the manatee and didn't really expect to, it had felt good to try. Especially since nobody else was doing anything.

Memaw went on, shaking her head: "I can't stop wondering who would do such a fool-brained thing."

I couldn't stop wondering, either. Might as well do something as sit around and wonder. "I expect I'll go back out tomorrow," I said.

"That's the way, Skeeter," said Memaw. "Stick to it. It's like my singing." She poked her hair modestly. "I have a certain amount of talent, Lord knows, He gave it to me Himself. But it was hard work and practice that won me that karaoke contest. Nobody ever got anywhere by giving up. Now, bring home your mama's supper, will you?"

I picked up the carton filled with Ten Thousand Delights and Memaw picked up the check. Then she reached for the menu and slipped it into her pocketbook. "I'm going to hang this on the refrigerator so I can think about what I'm going to order next time," she said. "There are still oodles of things we haven't tried yet."

There were oodles of places I hadn't looked for the manatee, too, and I guessed I was going to try them all.

Twelve

I spent most of Friday searching the shoreline out in the gulf. Saturday, I went back to searching the backcountry channels. It had been kind of fun the first time, but by the afternoon I decided that looking for a channel marker in a heavy fog would be a lot easier than the task I'd set myself. I was about to give up and forget the whole thing.

Then I spotted vultures circling in the sky.

I felt my heartbeat quicken and told myself to settle down. Sure, something beneath them was dead, but it wasn't necessarily the manatee. I counted the vultures. There were twelve. Whatever it was had to be pretty big to attract that large a crowd. I thought there were probably more on the ground, already feeding. The problem was getting to them. I figured they were a quarter to a half mile away, as the crow flies. But I had to find a water route, and that was going to be tricky.

It was. As the river heads to the ocean, it fans out into a lot of separate channels. There's one main channel out to the gulf, well marked so tourists can follow it. But there are a bunch of other, smaller routes to the sea, so that if you know the area and how much water your boat draws, there are lots of ways to go. Then there are about a gazillion smaller channels that branch off those channels, leading into the backcountry. While this made our river interesting, it sure made my job harder.

Keeping my eye on the vultures, I steered the boat down every little channel that appeared to lead in the right direction, but each route I took either came to an abrupt dead end or soon meandered away from where I wanted to go. Just as I began to be afraid that the tide would get too low for me to continue, I reached a large area of open, shallow water. At its far edge, I could see the hunched bodies of vultures feeding. I don't know why, but the sight of them hanging around like a bunch of ghouls made me angry. I shouted, "Get out! Get lost!"

The birds in the air rose higher and soared off as my skiff approached. The ones on the ground seemed reluctant to leave their feast, but I kept screaming at them, and one by one, with a lot of awkward hopping and wing flapping, they took off, too, leaving me alone with whatever it was they'd been eating. The smell wafted in my direction on the breeze.

I cut the engine and drifted over to the lumpy mass lying in the tangle of mangrove roots. The vultures had eaten some of the evidence, but even in its stinky, disgusting state, it was obvious that this was the manatee. I let out a whoop. It was totally gross, but I'd actually found it!

The birds had opened up its belly to feed, and I tried not to look at that part but at the head and face, which were clearly visible. Tied around its neck was a circle of blue nylon rope.

I stood still, trying to push away the rush of thoughts that crowded my brain at the sight of that blue rope. I'd seen that same blue line—or, rather, a coil of line like it—just days before, in the bottom of Dirty Dan's boat. After nearly slipping on it, I'd stowed it in the front storage compartment.

Where the gun was.

I leaned out of the skiff, picked up the end of the rope, and held it in my palm to feel its heft. It was the same weight line, I was sure. It was made of the same blue nylon.

So what? I asked myself. *Line like that is for sale at Larry's, where anybody can buy it off a huge spool.* I looked at it more closely. It was old and frayed and discolored where the sun had beaten down on it, just like the rope in the bottom of Dan's boat. *But that could have happened to a rope lying in anyone's boat or on anyone's dock. Just because there's a piece of it around the manatee's neck doesn't prove anything.*

And what exactly was I trying to prove, anyway? Dirty Dan was the Tarpon Man. He was my hero. He was not a manatee killer. So what if he called manatees "live speed bumps." He was only fooling around, griping, as Earl had said. The whole idea that he'd kill a manatee was ridiculous. *I* was ridiculous. My imagination was way out of control.

Then I remembered the ball. At the scene of the crime, I'd picked up trash for my still-life project in art class. Among those pieces of trash was a ball, a fairly new yellow tennis ball. I hadn't thought anything about it at the time. But now, in my mind's eye, I saw Blink reaching into his pocket for a bright yellow tennis ball to throw for Blinky. Blink, who never went anywhere without a quarter for me to flip for him and a yellow tennis ball for Blinky to chase. Blink, who was Dirty Dan's son.

Blink, or maybe Blinky, could have dropped the ball in the boat, and it could have fallen out when Dan was working to hide his tracks. Or maybe Blink and Blinky had been with him in the boat that day.

It didn't really matter. Take the rope or the ball or the gun one at a time, and they could mean anything. Put them all together, and—*No!* I told myself. *There's got to be another way to look at this.*

I thought back to the day I'd found the manatee. I tried to recall Dan's reaction to the news. He'd been at the River Haven Grill when Mac, Earl, and I had first discussed it. As far as I could remember, Dan hadn't said anything. He hadn't acted surprised and outraged like everybody else.

Because he already knew? Suddenly, I remembered the feeling of being watched when I was standing by the manatee's body that morning. *Had* I been seen? By Dirty Dan?

He had listened to my story, and then he'd asked me if I wanted to go tarpon fishing with him.

At the time, I'd been too thrilled to ask myself why. But now I wondered: Why had Dirty Dan the Tarpon Man asked me *then*, on that particular day, when I'd been dying to go fishing with him for as long as I could remember? And why *me*? I'd figured it was because I was Mac's son, and had even dared to suppose it was because Dan liked me and thought I was finally a good enough fisherman to catch a tarpon.

But what if he was only trying to keep me from thinking about the dead manatee? What if he was trying to get on my good side, in case I did somehow discover the terrible thing he had done?

Of course that was it. Why would Dirty Dan spend a whole day poling me around after tarpon? What did he get out of it . . . except the hope that I wouldn't discover what a slimeball he was, or, if I did, that I'd be too awed or too grateful to do anything about it? He'd played me for a fool, and I'd fallen for it.

I sat in the skiff, my head in my hands, as alternating surges of anger and humiliation—and doubt—passed through me. What was I doing? I couldn't just condemn Dirty Dan, who was Mac's good friend and who had helped me catch my first tarpon on a fly. I had to be sure.

Then I thought of a way. I reached into my pocket for my penknife. Trying not to gag, I leaned close over the manatee's body and cut the rope from around its neck. Sawing through the line several times, I made eight small pieces. I pocketed both of the end pieces, one of which Dan—*or someone else*, I reminded myself—had cut from a larger coil. Then, at each turn that I came to as I worked my way back out toward the river, I tied a piece of rope onto a branch of a mangrove tree. Like Hansel and Gretel's bread crumbs, the scraps of blue rope would mark my path back to the manatee. I wasn't going to lose my proof again.

There was just enough high water so that I made it to the river without getting stuck. Motoring up to Larry's, I prayed that I wouldn't run into Dirty Dan there. I didn't know what I'd do if I came face-to-face with him. I had to be sure before

I saw him. Then, when all my suspicions turned out to be wrong, maybe I'd tell him about it and we'd have a good laugh.

I tied up my own skiff, and looked over at Dan's slip. His boat was there. Looking around again, I saw no sign of Dirty Dan, and, thank goodness, for once Blink wasn't around, either.

Feeling as if *I* were the criminal, I crept down the dock and into Dan's boat. I opened the front storage compartment. The molded plastic gun case and the gun were gone. But the coil of rope was there. From my pocket I took the two pieces I'd cut from the manatee's neck.

I held one up to the end of the large coil. The strands met where they had been cut with a knife. They matched perfectly.

Thirteen

At home, there was a note on the refrigerator from Memaw. It was hanging right next to the menu from the Golden Moon Chinese restaurant, which I saw every time I got a snack or a glass of milk. The sentence "THE CUSTOMER IS BOOS" always caught my eye and cracked me up, but not now.

Memaw's note said that she was shopping and would be home soon, and that Mom had to work late because somebody was sick. In a way, I was relieved that I didn't have to talk to either of them—or to anybody—yet. But I could hardly stand being alone with my thoughts. I paced from the living room to the kitchen and back, Dirty Dan's treachery burning in my stomach like a hot stone.

I went to my bedroom and took out my backpack, where I'd put my still-life objects for art class. I dumped them all out on my bed, and examined the tennis ball closely. It looked as if it had been chewed on, but I couldn't be sure.

Staring blindly at the pile of stuff on my bed, I wondered how the man I'd seen tenderly releasing a tarpon back into the water could be the same man who put a bullet into the head of a harmless manatee.

None of it made sense.

When Memaw came home, I was glad to have a break from my repetitive, useless thoughts. I helped her bring the groceries in from the car. "Your mama's madder than spit that she's ended up having to work extra on a day when you've got vacation," she said as we were putting away the food. "She said to tell you she's sorry."

"It's okay," I murmured.

"It's that new employee, Veronica," Memaw declared. "She calls in sick every time she has a hangnail, I swear. Now, what shall we make ourselves for supper, Skeeter? Are you in the mood for tuna fish, or maybe your Memaw's world-famous macaroni and cheese?"

I tried to rouse myself and pay attention. "What? Oh. I don't know."

"Well, if you don't know, who does?"

I shrugged. "Either one's fine, I guess."

Memaw put her hands on her hips and gave me a penetrating look. "Either you've gone and fallen in love or something's troubling you. Which one is it?"

I looked up at her, surprised.

"Your mind is a thousand miles away, Skeeter. You think I can't tell when I'm talking to a fence post?"

"Sorry," I said. Then I thought about her question. "*In love*? Who would I be in love with?"

"That's what I was hoping you'd tell me," Memaw said, lifting her eyebrows and grinning. "Now that I've got your attention."

I shook my head and grinned back. "Sorry, Memaw, it's nothing like that." Then I felt my smile fade.

"So, something *is* wrong."

"Yeah."

"Is it that paper for your English teacher?"

"No. Way worse than that."

Memaw's expression grew serious. Before she could ask, I blurted out, "I found the manatee."

"Well, good for you, darlin'!" she exclaimed. "That's wonderful!" She looked at me again and asked uncertainly, "Isn't it?"

I let out a big sigh. It seemed I talked more to Memaw than to anybody else these days. Which was okay. I mean, Memaw was good to talk to, and whatever she had to say, she always gave it to you straight, and I liked that. But in a weird way, I didn't want to tell her what I'd found out, because telling her would make it really true. Even while I knew Dan had to be the killer, part of me couldn't accept it. I wanted to go back to not knowing, but that was something I'd never be able to do.

"Dirty Dan did it," I said at last. It came out as a whisper. I said, louder, "Dirty Dan is the killer."

Memaw looked surprised. Then her expression grew grave. She pulled two stools from under the kitchen counter and sat on one. Still looking at me, she gestured for me to take the other.

My legs suddenly felt too weak to hold me up, and I fell gratefully onto the stool. My shoulders slumped, and I leaned forward, my face in my hands. "I can't believe it," I said as hot tears slipped from between my fingers.

Memaw didn't say anything right away. She waited until I'd got hold of myself. When I raised my head and wiped my shirtsleeve over my face, she said, "Tell me what happened, Skeeter."

I told her everything, not even caring that now Mom would find out about the gun being in the boat, and all the rest of it. Because it turned out Mom had been right about Dirty Dan. No, that wasn't exactly true. She didn't know the half of how truly dirty Dan was.

After I'd finished, Memaw was quiet again for a while before she finally spoke. "What are you going to do?" she asked.

"I don't *know*," I said. "I'd tell Mac, except he's down in the Keys." After a moment I said, "I guess I could tell Earl." As soon as I'd said it, it seemed to be the obvious answer. Let the police handle it.

Memaw nodded. "Telling Earl's one possibility," she agreed. "Or . . ." She paused before continuing.

I looked up, the question in my eyes.

"You could talk to Dan first."

I stared at Memaw, puzzled. "But—why?" I asked.

"To hear his side of the story, of course."

"But what could he possibly say that would make a difference?" I said.

"Ask him," Memaw said. When I looked at her in confusion, she said, "Look, Skeet, you liked Dan, right? You liked him a lot."

"But that was before—"

"Just let me finish here. What about the things you liked him for? Did they all change?"

My head was spinning. "Are you saying because Dirty Dan is a great fisherman and helped me catch a tarpon, that makes it okay that he killed the manatee?"

Memaw shook her head. "No, Skeeter," she said, and her voice was softer than usual. "All I'm saying is that if the man was your friend, you might want to go to him first, before you go to the law. I'd want a friend of mine to do that, wouldn't you?"

Well, yeah, I thought. I guessed I would. But I'd never actually thought of Dan as *my* friend. He was Mac's friend, and Memaw's. He was a grownup, an adult. I couldn't just go over to his house and accuse him, even though he deserved it. I didn't have any idea what to say to him.

On the other hand, I had to do something soon. The vultures would make short work of what was left of the manatee, and that was my main evidence, along with the rope and ball and gun.

"So you think I should go over there and—and say *what*?"

I wanted Memaw to tell me exactly what to do, but all she said was, "Up to you, Skeeter. It's only four o'clock, so there's plenty of time before we'll be ready to eat." She began puttering around the kitchen, taking out what she'd need to make supper.

I sat there, and the more I thought about what Memaw had said about talking to Dan, the more it seemed the right thing to do. If I ran to Earl, I'd be tattling, something a mad, scared kid would do. Talking to Dan, man to man, felt more grownup.

"Okay. I'll go." I said the words even as my mind was screaming, *But you* are *just a kid! And you* are *mad—and scared, too!*

"Let me get my purse," said Memaw.

"You're coming?" I asked in surprise.

"I believe you've made a good decision, Skeeter. But you don't think I'm going to let you go by yourself, do you?"

I was embarrassed by the flood of relief I felt.

"I've known Dan for a long time, Skeet, and I think he deserves to be heard," Memaw went on. "But he might be a lawbreaker, and we know he has a gun, and I'm not taking any chances with my only grandchild. You ready?"

I nodded dumbly, and followed her to the car. I was so glad I wasn't going to have to confront Dirty Dan, after all. Memaw was going to be there, and she'd know what to say. She drove into the back lot at Larry's and pulled up in front of Dan's camper. I opened my car door and started to get out.

"Good luck, Skeeter, darlin'," Memaw said.

I stopped, stunned. "Aren't you coming?"

"I'll be right here if you need me," she said brightly.

"But, I—"

"Talk to the man, Skeet," she said, reaching over to squeeze my hand.

As I walked toward the camper, I imagined myself saying to Dan, "Now, don't try anything. I brought my grandmother, and she's right outside."

I pictured Memaw hitting Dirty Dan over the head with her purse. It might have been funny if I hadn't been so scared.

I stood at the door, thinking I wouldn't even have to knock because Dan could surely hear the pounding of my heart.

Fourteen

A moment later Dan was at the door, his scar stretching wide with his smile. "Well, if it isn't the Tarpon Kid," he said. "Come on in, Skeet."

I almost found myself smiling back, the way I would have in the old days. But I caught myself, remembering that everything had changed. So I just stood there like a dope.

"Blink," Dan called into the camper. "Come see who's here."

Blink came running to the door, followed by Blinky. When he saw me, Blink's face lit up and his hand went for his pocket. We played a few rounds of our game right then and there, with me still standing on the cinder block they used for a step.

I'd noticed Dan looking out toward Memaw's car while Blink and I played flip. "That your grandma out there in the car?" he asked when we were done.

I nodded.

"She want to come in?" he asked.

"No."

Dan looked puzzled and said, "Well, how 'bout you? No sense in us standing here letting all the air-conditioning out."

The moment had come, but I was so nervous I was shaking. After taking a deep breath, I managed to say, "I've got to talk to you."

"So come on in," he said, stepping back so I could pass through the door.

I glanced toward Blink. I said quietly so he couldn't hear, "Alone would probably be better."

Dan nodded. Calmly, he turned to Blink and said, "Could you eat a slice of that red-and-white cardboard Larry calls pizza?"

Blink laughed and laughed with delight. "It's not cardboard, Dirty Dan! Dirty Dan is silly! Blinky likes Larry's pizza and so do I. Skeeter, do you like Larry's pizza?"

I nodded, trying to smile back at him. I wished

I could leave and go to Larry's with him, even if it meant eating a piece of the awful stuff that came out of Larry's microwave.

"Here," said Dan, reaching into his wallet and handing Blink two dollars. "One slice for you and one for Blinky. Then come on home, okay?"

"Okay, Dirty Dan. One for me and one for Blinky. Thanks, Dirty Dan. Bye, Skeet."

"See ya, Blink," I said miserably. I'd suddenly thought of something. What would Blink do if Dirty Dan went to jail? I pushed the thought away.

Blink was gone and I was face-to-face with Dan. I didn't have much time. If Larry wasn't busy, Blink could get two slices of pizza nuked and be back in five minutes.

Dan nodded toward a chair, and sat in what was obviously his usual seat in front of the TV. He took the bottle of Jack Daniel's from the table and poured some into a glass. "Get you something to drink?" he asked.

I shook my head.

Dan took a long sip. "Well?" he said. "Somehow I get the feeling you're not here to talk about tarpon fishing, the weather, or the price of tea in China."

I swallowed. After a pause I spoke, and the

words came out in a rush. "I found the manatee's body. There was a blue rope around its neck. It matches the rope in your boat."

Dan lifted an eyebrow, and his scar stretched upward. He took a sip from the glass and looked at me, waiting for me to say more.

"And at the place where I first saw the manatee, there was one of Blinky's tennis balls. I have it." Then I stared into my lap, unable to look at him. This time, I waited for him to speak.

The silence in the little camper grew until it became excruciating. I wanted to scream, *Say something!* Finally I said desperately, "I saw your gun."

He nodded, sipped, and said, "And that led you to conclude what, exactly?"

Oh, man. He was doing this on purpose, trying to make it even harder for me! Did I have to spell it all out? Couldn't he just admit what he'd done? My anger gave me enough courage to say, "You're the one. You shot it. Then you hid it."

Dan looked somewhere over my shoulder for a long time without speaking.

"Why?" I whispered at last.

"Why," Dan repeated, and he sounded very tired. He didn't offer an answer to the question. After another long silence he said, "Remember on Wednesday, how you looked and looked for fish and at first you couldn't see them, even though they were right there the whole time?"

What's he doing, talking about fishing? I thought wildly.

He went on. "And then you began to look through the water, not just at the surface, and you began to see?"

He was trying to change the subject. Trying to make me think about something else. How simple did he think I was? "Yeah," I said, sounding and feeling angry. "So what?"

"All I'm saying is that things aren't always the way they look at first." He shrugged and took a sip from his glass.

"That's *it*?" I said. I couldn't believe it. "That's all you have to say?"

Dan set the glass down. "Until you cool off and have a chance to think this over, I guess it is," he answered.

I stood up, furious. What was there to think over? I could feel how red my face was. I was conscious of my hands and legs shaking, and my heart beating way too fast. I knew how I must look to Dirty Dan, and that only made everything worse.

In my mind I was shouting, *Until I cool off? What's that supposed to mean? Until I'm as cool, no, as cold-blooded as you?* I wanted to say, *You let people call you the Tarpon Man, Mr. Catch-and-Release Fisherman, but maybe you never noticed—it's a little hard to release something after it has a bullet through its brain!*

That was what I wanted to say. It was what I should have said. It was what I *would* have said if I'd had any guts. Instead I stood there for a moment, sputtering mad, while Dirty Dan sat in his chair with an expression on his face that I couldn't read.

Then I tore open the door of the camper and ran out, nearly tripping on the cinder-block step as I made my escape. Blink was just coming across the yard from Larry's, his face smeared with pizza sauce. The happy grin fell from his face as I pushed on by.

"Uh-oh," I heard him say. His voice rose in the high, panicky way it did when he sensed trouble. "Uh-oh, Blinky. Skeet's mad now. Uh-oh. Uh-oh. Oh, boy."

I could have stopped to tell him not to worry, that I wasn't mad at him. But I didn't do that, either. I got into the car and slammed the door shut. Memaw looked at me questioningly, but I didn't explain and she didn't press me.

When we got home, I headed to my room.

"Not hungry?" Memaw asked.

I shook my head.

"I expect you've got some thinking to do," she said.

I nodded.

"If you feel like company, I'll be right here," she said.

"Thanks," I said dully, though I was thankful that she knew when to leave a person alone.

Lying on my bed, I stared at the ceiling while I went over and over my meeting with Dirty Dan. There was one thing he had said that I had to admit was true: things really *aren't* always the way they look at first. For years, I had thought Dan was a hero.

Fifteen

It was Sunday morning, the last day of spring break. I lay in bed, thinking that this vacation had brought both the best and the worst days of my life. I felt tired, and I hadn't even gotten up yet. When I remembered that it was also the last day to do my stupid assignment for English, I pulled the pillow over my head and wriggled down farther under the covers.

Mom knocked, then came in and sat on the end of my bed. "Morning, sweetie," she said. "You were already asleep when I got home last night."

"Yeah. I was zonked." I wondered whether Memaw had told her about Dirty Dan. If so, maybe Mom was going to tell me what I should do.

But what she said was, "I have to go into work again, Skeet. I can't believe it. Veronica is still claiming to be sick, and I've got no one else to cover for her. I was hoping we could do something together today, something special, since I've hardly seen you this past week."

"It's okay," I said.

"It isn't okay, but there's nothing I can do about it," she said with a sigh. Then, giving me a wistful little smile, she asked, "So, what are your plans for the day?"

"I don't know." Boy, was that the truth.

"Well, Memaw will be around if you need anything. I should be able to get out at five o'clock, if nothing else goes wrong."

"Okay."

"And, Skeet?" She looked down at her lap for a minute, then raised her eyes to meet mine. "About what you overheard me saying to your father the other morning? When he gets back from the Keys, we'll all three talk about it, all right?"

I shrugged. She wasn't really asking me, so I didn't really answer.

She leaned over to pat my leg under the covers. "Until then, you just try not to worry about it."

"Sure, Mom."

"No matter what happens, your father and I both love you more than anything."

"I know. But—"

"But what, honey?"

"Don't you love Mac anymore?"

She sighed. "It's not that simple, Skeet. I think he's a good person. It's just hard for me to live with him. We're so different. I'm sure you can see that."

"Well, yeah. But that's the way you've always been. Why does everything have to change all of a sudden?"

Mom sighed. "It's not really all of a sudden. It's— Well, it's very complicated." She tried unsuccessfully to smile.

I swung my legs off the bed and got to my feet, tired of questions nobody could answer. Mom sat on the bed for a minute, looking as if she wanted to say more. Then she, too, got up. I went to the kitchen and she went to her room to get dressed for work.

Memaw was at the stove when I walked in. "I'm in the mood for bacon, Skeet, how about you?"

The smell coming from the sizzling pan was

tantalizing. I remembered I hadn't eaten dinner the night before. "You bet!" I said.

"I knew I could count on you, Skeet. I don't know how your mama eats that hamster food she calls cereal every morning. She says it's good for her cholesterol, but I'm not sure a human body is meant to digest twigs and pellets. I like a breakfast with a little flavor myself. How about we have some eggs to go with this?"

"Yeah!"

"Fried or scrambled?"

"Fried, sunny-side up."

"You got it, mister. Now, if you'll put some of that bread in the toaster and pour us some orange juice, we'll be all set."

We were just digging in when Mom came through the kitchen to say goodbye. After we heard her car pull out of the driveway, I asked Memaw about something that had been troubling me. "Memaw, what would happen to Blink if Dan had to go to jail?"

She seemed to consider this while she sopped up the last of her egg with a piece of toast. "Why, I don't really know. I imagine Blink would get sent to some sort of facility where they care for people like him."

"Would they let him keep Blinky at a place like that?" I asked.

She set down her fork. "I don't know, Skeet," she said. She added sadly, "Probably not."

We didn't say anything for a while. Then Memaw said quietly, "Life has a way of getting complicated, doesn't it, darlin'?"

I nodded. "Mom just said the same thing."

"I take it Dan didn't deny doing the shooting?" Memaw asked.

"He told me to cool off and think it over!" I told her, feeling outraged all over again. "That's all I've been doing—thinking about it! And all I do is go around in circles. Dan shouldn't get away with it. But if I tell Earl, he'll have to investigate, even though Dan's his friend. When he finds out everything I know, Dan will be in big trouble."

Memaw nodded. "And trouble for Dan means trouble for Blink. It's not fair, but there it is."

I said miserably, "I wish I'd never found the stupid manatee in the first place. But now I have to do something, and whatever I do seems wrong—including not doing anything!" I groaned and pushed my plate away, the sight of the yellow remains making me feel sick.

Memaw cleared the table and sat down again. "I don't see any harm in taking Dan's advice," she said thoughtfully. I must have looked incredulous, because she added quickly, "I don't mean the part about cooling off. I think you're right to be hot and bothered about a harmless creature being shot like that. But it's too late to save the manatee, so why not take your time and think over your options?"

"Well, for one thing, the body disappeared once and I'm afraid it'll disappear again," I said. "For all I know, Dan might have already gone out this morning and towed it way out in the gulf, tied a cinder block to it, and chucked it overboard."

Memaw stirred her coffee and said, "If he has, there's nothing you can do about it now. And if he hasn't, he probably won't, and you've got nothing to lose by waiting. It'll give you a chance to talk it all over with your mama and Mac."

"Yeah, *right*," I said.

Memaw's eyebrows arched up, probably at the anger in my voice, which surprised even me.

I added, "Mac's in the Keys and Mom's at work,

and besides, how can I talk about anything with them? There's no *them* anymore."

Memaw didn't disagree, or say any of the stupid things grownups often say to comfort kids, and which kids know aren't true. She just nodded, looking sad. "Your mama and Mac are having a hard time," she said. "But I imagine it's harder on you than on anybody."

"I don't understand what was wrong with the way things were before," I said, and I could hear the tears in my voice, ready to spill out.

Memaw didn't say anything; she just made a sympathetic sound. After a moment she said, "There was a lot of fighting before Mac left. They tried to hide it, but I'm sure you heard it, too."

"Yeah," I said. I realized I'd heard it and not heard it at the same time, because I hadn't *wanted* to. "I mean, I know Mom and Mac are *different* . . ." I let the sentence trail away.

Memaw nodded. "It was his easygoing, happy-go-lucky charm that attracted your mama to him in the first place, I think," she said. "But more and more, that's what annoys and upsets her. And Mac can't understand why she isn't able to relax and be more like him. If only they could meet in the middle. But that's not the way they're made. Right now they think they're doing what's best for them—and for you."

"That's stupid!" I said. "If they really want what's best for me, why don't they ask me?"

"What would you tell them?"

"I'd tell them to make everything like it was before."

Memaw sighed and reached across the table to cover my hand with her cool, dry one. "I know how you feel, Skeeter, honey. But life doesn't ever let us go backwards, much as we want to sometimes."

We stayed that way for a while, and I liked the feel of Memaw's hand on mine. I thought about what she'd said. Wishing Mom and Mac would be the way they were before was like wishing I'd never found the manatee. It was too late for that.

Finally, Memaw squeezed my fingers and leaned back. "I'd feel a lot better if you'd talk with your parents about this business with Dan, Skeet. I can't help thinking there's another answer here somewhere. What do you say we tell your mama when she gets home, and then you can call your daddy on his cell phone. Four heads are better than two, I always say."

I had to admit I felt relief at the idea of Memaw, Mac, and Mom sharing in my decision about what to do. I didn't like the possibility that the evidence could disappear again—if it hadn't already—but at least I could check on that. I couldn't count on Memaw being right that it probably wouldn't.

"Okay," I said. After a moment, I added, "Thanks, Memaw." I was grateful to her, and I felt really bad about the lie I was about to tell her.

Sixteen

Memaw would never have agreed to it, but I had to make sure the manatee's body was still there. I crossed my fingers on both hands when I told her I was going over to my friend Lenny's house, knowing I'd never said anything about Lenny visiting his grandparents.

"Well, good, Skeet," she said. "That'll help keep your mind off this business with Dan."

I was washing the frying pan and the dishes, too, without even being asked, and Memaw shot me a probing look. "I don't need to call Lenny's mama, do I?"

"No, ma'am," I said, as innocently as I could. Inside I was thinking, *Please, no!*

"You wouldn't be thinking of doing anything foolish, would you?"

"Absolutely not," I assured her. I felt like a first-class creep, but I told myself it *wasn't* foolish to check on the manatee; it was plain common sense. To change the subject, I said, "I'll be home by five. That's when Mom said she'd get out of work."

"All right," Memaw said. "Then we'll get to the bottom of this mess."

I sure hoped so. Meanwhile, I'd make certain that nothing happened to the evidence, in case we needed it. I told myself again that there was no need for Memaw to know. It would only give her something to worry about.

When I got to the marina, I looked first to see if Dirty Dan's boat was in its slip. It was. Either he'd already gone out, dumped the manatee, and returned, or the evidence was safe.

Blink and Blinky came running over as I headed down the dock to my skiff. Blink's hand reached for the quarter, and we played our game.

"So, what's Dirty Dan up to today?" I asked casually.

A shadow passed across Blink's normally sunny face. His forehead wrinkled with worry, and his eyes started blinking like mad. He glanced back over his shoulder toward the little camper. "Uh-oh," he said. "Uh-oh. Dirty Dan said watch out for Skeet. Be careful if Skeet asks questions. That's what Dirty Dan said. Be careful. Uh-oh. Uh-oh. Was I careful, Skeet?"

"You were real careful, Blink," I said quickly.

"I told Dirty Dan I could keep quiet," Blink said anxiously. "I told him I was quiet in the boat. I was quiet in the boat, wasn't I, Skeet?"

"Sure, Blink," I said, having no idea what he was talking about, but wanting to reassure him. "Don't worry. Look, Blinky wants to play. You'd better go throw the ball for Blinky now, okay?"

"I'll go throw the ball for Blinky now, okay, Skeet?"

"Good," I said, edging away, not wanting Dirty Dan to look out and see Blink talking to me. "You were real careful, Blink," I called back. "Real quiet. Don't worry."

I got into my skiff and yanked angrily on the cord to start the motor. Nothing happened. I yanked four or five more times before I realized the choke was out. The motor flooded and stalled. I took a deep breath and tried to settle down. Poor

Blink. Dan was trying to keep him from talking to me, and had gotten him all frightened and confused. Blink would be better off in some sort of facility, I thought furiously, where he'd be safe from Dirty Dan.

The engine finally started, and I headed down the river, forcing myself to control my speed through the refuge area, wishing I were old enough or brave enough to go rescue Blink right then and there. As it was, I had to content myself with hoping that something would be done soon. At least I could make sure we still had the evidence we'd need to finish this once and for all.

When I got to the backcountry channels, I was glad to see the tide was still high enough for my boat to maneuver. I found the first blue rope marker and followed it to the next marker, and the next, and the next. Soon I saw a lone vulture circling in the sky overhead, and came to the open stretch of water where the other vultures were gathered to feed. I approached slowly, and they seemed more reluctant than before to leave their feast. I drew quite close before they rose to make an awkward escape.

Little was left of the carcass—that was the word

that came to my mind when I saw it this time, not *manatee*, or even *body*, but *carcass*. There was enough to tell that it had once been a manatee. Enough, no doubt, for an expert to identify the hole in its skull as a bullet wound. Enough to nail Dirty Dan.

I was thinking all this when suddenly a noise made its way into my consciousness, causing my heart to lurch. I sat up straight, my full attention focused on the sound. Different from the buzzing of the flies, it was a low, steady humming. A boat engine. Maybe a quarter mile away, but coming closer. I strained to listen and, yes, it was definitely coming closer. Which meant it had left the main river and was coming into the backcountry. Coming steadily closer, not hesitating, not changing direction, not stopping to fish. Coming steadily through the maze of channels directly toward where I sat. It had to be a small skiff like mine, or a flats boat—something that didn't draw a lot of water.

It was someone who knew exactly where he was going. I sat there, paralyzed, hypnotized by the steady humming sound and the glare of the sun on the water and the moist heat that threatened to suffocate me. It didn't matter. There was nowhere to go. I was trapped at the far end of that little back-country channel like a crab in a bait tank.

I forced myself out of my panicked stupor and tried to think, and the first thought I had was a bad one. I had no radio. The second thought was worse. Memaw thought I was at Lenny's. She didn't expect me home until five o'clock. No one knew where I was.

No one, I realized as the boat appeared around the bend, except Dirty Dan.

Seventeen

Dirty Dan motored slowly across the open stretch of water toward where I sat in my skiff, frozen with panic and a weird sense that this couldn't really be happening. It seemed to take hours for him to reach me, hours during which my mind scrambled frantically for a way out and came up with nothing.

Dan cut the engine at the right moment to allow his boat to glide alongside mine. The silence was complete. There wasn't the squawk of a bird, the buzz of an insect, or the splash of a fish in the shallow water. It was as if Dan and I were alone at the end of the world.

Finally he spoke. "Hello, Skeet."

I didn't answer. My throat felt so dry I wasn't sure I could.

"We need to have a talk."

I still didn't—couldn't—answer.

After a moment, he gestured toward the manatee. "You couldn't let it go, could you? Had to keep after it." Then he nodded, saying, "I understand that. You're stubborn. It's the same stubbornness that made you keep trying until you caught that tarpon. I got it, too."

He smiled at me, his scar stretching in his brown, leathery face, and he seemed so much like the old Dan I almost smiled back. I caught myself and looked away.

"But now we got ourselves a situation, Skeet, and one of us is going to have to give in. I came out here to see who it was going to be, you or me."

At last I found my voice, though it came out kind of small and croaky. "What if I won't give in? Are you going to kill me, too?"

Dan shook his head, and even though I knew better, I thought he looked genuinely sad. "I guess I can't blame you for thinking like that, Skeet, but it pains me all the same." He sighed. "I saw you talking to Blink this morning. He came home all nervous and upset again, and I knew I had to do something to stop—all this. I didn't come to hurt you. I came so nobody and nothing else gets hurt." He pointed to the manatee and made a wry face. "It's too late for him."

"Yeah," I said. "Thanks to you. Now you want me to keep quiet about it, just so you don't have to answer for what you did?"

"In a way, yes."

I couldn't believe it. He sure had nerve, I had to give him credit for that.

Dan went on, "Because, in a way, it really *was* my fault."

Oh, really? I thought, almost letting loose a wild laugh. *Next you're going to tell me that, in another way, it was the manatee's fault for getting in the path of the bullet you shot at him!*

"I never should have let Blink shoot the gun," Dan said.

What? Blink and a gun?

"But we were pretty far out in the boonies that morning, and there was nobody else around, and I thought, what harm could it do? He'd been after me for a long time to shoot the gun, saying he just wanted to try it. Probably because of things he sees on TV." Dan's voice trailed off for a second.

"Anyway, there were a few of Blinky's old tennis balls rolling around the bottom of the boat, so I told Blink I'd throw them out and he could shoot at them. I showed him the right way to hold the gun and how to work the safety, and told him never to point it at anyone. Told him he could shoot at three balls in the water. Just that one time, I said."

Dan looked away, then back at me, and said, "There are so many things he can't do, you know? I thought I could let him do this, let him feel like a regular kid for once . . . It seemed harmless enough at the time."

Dan was quiet for a minute, and I thought I could see how letting Blink shoot at some tennis balls might have sounded like an okay idea.

Then Dan said, "So he was real careful and he shot at one, then another . . . missing, you know, but laughing and getting a big kick out of the noise and the splash and all. And then, just as I threw the third ball, this manatee's head popped up out of the water, and before I knew it, he'd shot it." Dan paused, and shrugged.

I didn't say a word, I was so caught up in the

story, picturing it in my mind: the dopey manatee's head coming up and Blink, taken by surprise, pulling the trigger before he even knew what he was doing, hitting the manatee in the head.

Echoing my thoughts, Dan said, "I'm sure he didn't know what he was doing. At first he was excited because the manatee drifted over near the boat and he could touch it. He didn't understand why it wasn't moving. When I told him it was dead, he got all worked up, you know how he does, crying and all. I still don't know if he understands that he shot it."

No, I thought, *you can't ever be sure, not with Blink.*

"And I didn't try to make him understand. It would only make him feel worse." Dan smiled weakly and said, "I guess there is one good thing that came out of all this. He doesn't want to play with the gun anymore."

I think I might have smiled back.

"Anyway, I was telling myself that it was an unfortunate accident, but it was an *accident*, and I couldn't see any good coming from Blink being hauled in and questioned or whatever might happen to him. I knew Earl would be good to him, but what if it wasn't Earl I was dealing with? Then I thought about saying I shot it, but if *I* was hauled in, then where would Blink be? I'm all he's got."

"Yeah," I said. "I know."

"Well, there's something you probably don't know, Skeet, and it made a difference in all this." He took off his hat, brushed his hand through his sweaty hair, and put the cap back on. "I've got a little problem with Mr. Jack Daniel's."

At first, I didn't know who he was talking about. Then I remembered: Jack Daniel's whiskey was his butterfly milk.

"Oh," I said.

"There was a time when I used to get blind, crazy drunk, get in fights, cause all kinds of trouble. I drove my wives away and got myself a record with the police. Then one night I got in a car accident when I was drunk as a skunk. Blink was in the car with me and he got banged up pretty good." Dan paused and looked down at his hands. "They almost took him away from me after that. Ever since then, I try to drink just enough to keep it together, keep my hands from shaking, you know?"

I didn't know, and I swallowed, not sure what to say. I thought about Dan sipping on the bottle all day in the boat, but not seeming drunk. I guessed that was what he meant, but I'd have to ask Mac or Memaw about it.

"So anyway, when I heard a boat coming that morning, all that stuff ran through my head. I guess I panicked, thinking Blink would get in trouble for shooting the manatee, or else I'd be in trouble for letting him. Maybe they'd take him away from me for real this time. Maybe there'd be a hefty fine, and I don't have the money for that. If I couldn't pay, maybe I'd go to jail. My past record wouldn't help. Maybe—well, like I said, I panicked. When I heard a boat coming, I poled my boat up a side channel and hid real quick.

"I never imagined it would be you, or that you'd find the body. But you did and— Well, here we are."

I thought of Blink talking about how quiet he'd been in the boat. Now I knew he was talking about staying quiet while he and Dan hid from me. Piecing the rest together, I said, "And then you went back and moved the body after I left to get Earl."

Dan nodded. "I didn't know for sure where you were going or if you'd be coming back, but the way you were examining the head, I knew you'd figured out it was shot."

"But Earl and I never saw you," I said. Then I realized, "Oh! You must have taken one of the smaller channels on the way back to the marina. That's why we didn't run into you on the river."

He nodded again.

And then neither of us said anything for a pretty long time. I was thinking about what Memaw had said that morning about life getting complicated, and it seemed, as usual, that she was right.

I was thinking about life giving you the down and dirty, and never letting you go backwards, and how that didn't just mean me and Mac and Mom, but Dirty Dan and Blink, too.

I was thinking, too, about parents loving their kids more than anything, and how that might make them do all sorts of things. Like Dan hiding the manatee to protect Blink. Or like Mom wanting real bad for me to have a life she thought would be better than hers. Or like Mac moving to a trailer down the street so I didn't have to hear any more fighting.

I was thinking that even though some people

might say what Dirty Dan did was wrong, maybe there was another way to look at it. I figured he was simply being the best father to Blink he knew how to be. He wasn't perfect, but so what? I was beginning to realize that nobody was.

I was always making everybody into heroes or bad guys, but most people—even parents—were muddling around somewhere in the middle.

"Okay," I said to Dan. "I give."

He looked back at me, his scar stretching with his puzzled frown.

"I give," I repeated. "You said one of us had to."

He buried his face in his hands for a second, breathing a big sigh of relief, and only then did I realize how worried he'd been. He said, "I was hoping if I explained, you'd understand."

"I do."

He nodded, staring off into the distance for a moment. Then, his glance indicating the manatee, he asked, "Should we try to bury that thing?"

I looked up at the sky and pointed to the vultures, who were circling again, waiting. "Let's leave it," I said. "Vultures have to eat, too, I guess."

Eighteen

It was a day for surprises, that was for sure. I got another one that afternoon, when I told Memaw that Blink had shot the manatee.

She listened, and didn't even yell at me for not going to Lenny's, as I'd told her I was doing. When she'd heard the whole story, she smiled real big and nodded as if it was exactly what she'd expected to hear.

"I had a feeling there was something more to it, Skeeter," she said. "I couldn't get my mind around the idea that Dan would kill a manatee in cold blood. It didn't feel right somehow. He may look tough with that nasty old scar and all, but he's a squishy old marshmallow inside."

"Memaw," I said, "speaking of that scar, did Dan ever tell you the whole story of how he got it?"

She laughed. "Shoot, Skeeter, he didn't have to tell me. I was there."

I was about to pour myself a glass of milk, and when I heard that, I nearly dropped the carton. "You were *there*?" I held the milk carton suspended, my jaw probably hanging halfway to the floor.

Memaw laughed again, and patted her hair.

"What happened, Memaw? Tell me!"

"Oh, darlin', it was a long time ago."

"But you remember, right?" I asked.

"Like it was yesterday," she answered.

I nodded to urge her along.

"Oh my, we were young, Dan and I. Your Memaw wasn't always an old lady, believe it or not."

I nodded again, wanting to keep the story coming.

"We had just got out of high school, if you can imagine."

I knew Memaw and Dan were about the same age. I tried to imagine them as high school kids, but the picture I came up with in my mind was kind of fuzzy—and pretty funny.

"So what happened?" I begged.

"Well, it was graduation night," Memaw began. "A group of us seniors got together to kick up our heels one last time before we all went off to get jobs, or get married, or whatever we had planned.

"We were picnicking and swimming up at the springs. It wasn't like it is now, all commercialized and crowded with so many people and tour boats and all. It was almost like our own little private swimming hole. Hardly anybody knew about it except us locals.

"There were some other, older fellows there, and they'd built a campfire down the shore from us, and they were getting pretty rowdy.

"Well, it got late and pitch-dark. I don't remember why, but I walked away from our group a little ways."

Memaw stopped to pour herself a cup of coffee, and I sat down on the stool by the counter, dying for her to continue.

"Then, out of nowhere, it seemed, one of those older fellows showed up beside me and I saw right off he'd had much too much to drink. And, Skeeter, he wasn't talking—or acting—like a gentleman. I told him to get away from me, but he wouldn't listen. I called for help, and the boys from our group came running over.

"I was so relieved, thinking that would be the end of it, and we'd all just go home. But that older fellow had a little ax hanging from his belt. He'd been using it to cut tree branches for the campfire, we all saw him. Well, he took out that little ax and started swinging it around, and when he did that, all the boys backed off real quick. All except for Dan, bless his heart."

A little ax, I thought. *She's talking about the hatchet!*

You could have knocked me over with the feathers on a tarpon fly. The mysterious blonde, the cause of the hatchet fight I'd imagined so often, was *Memaw*! I could not believe it.

"Dan came to my rescue like a hero in a storybook," Memaw went on. "He got a horrible cut on his face, and when the fellow with the ax saw all that blood pouring down Dan's cheek and onto his shirt, well, he turned tail and ran like a rabbit. We took Dan to the hospital to get his face stitched up, and that was that." Memaw took a sip of her coffee and said, "I'll always feel responsible for that scar, and I've loved Danny Houlihan ever since."

Danny Houlihan? I laughed. I'd never heard him called anything but Dirty Dan.

When I'd recovered enough to speak, I asked her, "But if you love him, how come you don't marry him?" Then I remembered something and added excitedly, "I saw him kiss you after the karaoke contest! I bet he loves you, too."

Memaw had a good chuckle over that. "I believe he does, Skeet, in his way. But some men are the marrying kind, Skeeter, and some aren't, and I can tell you for a fact that Dan *isn't*. There's four women out there who used to be his wives who'd agree with that. I was young and foolish, but even then I had a hunch Dan would make a much better friend than husband."

I hardly knew what to say, I was so flummoxed by the news. I loved the story of Dan's scar more than ever now, knowing he got it fighting for Memaw.

"You know something else, Skeet?" Memaw said a while later as she was washing her coffee cup. "I believe your mama and daddy might be better at being friends, too, instead of husband and wife."

I thought about that for a bit. Somehow, the way Memaw put it, it didn't sound so terrible.

"Do you think you could live with that?" she asked.

"I guess I might have to," I said.

Memaw smiled at me. Then she put her hands on her hips and raised her eyebrows. "Now, young man, we have something else we need to talk about."

Uh-oh. I knew what was coming. "Aw, Memaw, I'm real sorry I lied to you about going to Lenny's."

"Apology accepted. But that's not what I was going to say."

"It wasn't?" My mind scrambled to think of what else I'd done that was bad.

"Your mama and daddy are so distracted right now, neither of them thought to ask you why you didn't radio for Earl when you found the manatee. But I've been wondering."

Before I could say anything, she went on.

"And my guess is that your radio's broken and you didn't want to tell your mama because it would cramp your style during your school break if you couldn't go out in your boat. Am I right?"

Memaw didn't miss much, I had to say that for her. "Yeah. It's the antenna," I confessed. "I only need eight more dollars and I can get a new one."

"Tell you what. I can't make heads or tails of the directions for setting up that karaoke machine. If you'll help me, I'll pay you ten dollars. You promise me you won't go back out in the boat until the radio works, and the whole thing can be our little secret."

"Deal!" I said, and I gave her a hug. "Let's do it right now."

I set up the amp, speakers, and microphone where Memaw wanted it in the living room. Then I showed her how to load the discs with the background music and song lyrics into the player. She got pretty excited when she saw that the kit came with five different discs, and that each one held fifty different songs. She especially liked the one that had country hits on it.

"Why, Skeeter, you're a mechanical genius!" she exclaimed when the music to a song called "Chattanooga Sugarbabe" began to play, and the words showed up on the screen.

We fooled around with the karaoke machine for a while. We were doing a duet of a song called "Crazy" when Mom came home and said that's exactly what we were.

Then she asked if I'd written my English paper

yet, and told me I had about an hour to work on it before supper. I went to my room. I'd thrown my artistic trash collection off the bed the night before, and the objects lay scattered on the floor. I started to pick them up to put them in my backpack, and I remembered Mrs. Rathbun telling us that when we had our things gathered, we should take a real close look at them. "Look hard," she kept saying. "Try to really *see* each object and its relation to the others. Look over, under, around, and through."

I tried it. At first I just saw the same pile of junk. But after staring at that stuff for a while, I began to see the different angles and textures. I began rearranging the objects, and I saw how each thing changed depending on where it was in the big picture that included all the others. It was kind of cool, really, and I thought trying to paint them might be fun.

The paper was due the next day. I *had* to get started on it. But I couldn't write about the manatee, as Memaw had suggested. I wasn't "peeved" anymore, for one thing. And the other thing was, I didn't want to. As Dan had said the day I caught my tarpon, "Some things just oughtta stay secret."

A weird little idea had been in the back of my

mind ever since Memaw and I went to the Golden Moon, and I decided to write about it. I finished the first draft right before Mom called me to dinner. Afterwards, I asked if I could ride my bike over to the marina. Memaw winked at me. I guessed she knew why I was going.

Larry didn't have the antenna I needed in stock, but he said he could get it in two days. Halfway home, I saw Earl driving toward me. He pulled over next to me in his police car and stopped, and suddenly I felt scared. What if the police had finally decided to do an investigation? Now that I'd made such a big thing out of the manatee, how could I get Earl to back off without betraying Dan?

Luckily, Earl spoke first. "Dan came to see me a while ago," he said quietly. "He told me what happened to the manatee. I guess he told you, too."

"Yeah," I said. Then, quickly, I asked, "What happens now? You're not going to—to *do* anything, are you? I mean, to Dan or to Blink?"

Earl gazed out at an inflatable raft with a bunch of kids in it passing on the river. "Police officers have a certain amount of discretion when it comes to enforcing the law, Skeet," he said slowly. "Do you know what that means?"

I shook my head. "Not really."

"Well, it means that sometimes I need to look not just at the crime but at all the circumstances surrounding that crime. And then I have to decide what course of action best serves the people I'm supposed to be protecting." He paused and added, "All afternoon, I've been asking myself, what good would it do to follow the letter of the law in this case?"

I thought I knew what he was getting at. But I needed to know for sure. "So what did you decide?" I asked.

"I think by now the vultures have pretty much taken care of the body, and what's left will soon sink down into the muck and disappear. And that's where it'll stay. That's what I think."

I nodded, and smiled.

"Case closed?" he asked.

"Case closed."

Epilogue

Here's the paper I handed in to Mr. Giordano. He wants me to change a few things, but mostly he seemed to like it. He wrote "very original" in the margin, and "good idea" and "I'd like to meet your Memaw."

When I showed that to Memaw, she told me to invite him to the next karaoke night at the River Haven Grill, 'cause she's planning on singing.

Skeet Waters
English/Mr. Giordano

MY PET PEEVE
or
THE SKEET WATERS GOLDEN MOON MENU
METHOD OF GROWING YOURSELF UP
(First Draft)

My pet peeve is the way grownups always ask kids, "What do *you* want to be when you grow up?" Half the time they just want to tell you what they think would be good for you. Or else they're being polite, waiting for you to say, "A doctor," or "A lawyer," or "A gravedigger," so they can say, "Oh, isn't that nice?" and go talk to somebody else.

But saying what job you'll have doesn't tell anything about who you'd really *be*. I mean, isn't it more important to know what *kind* of gravedigger you would be? Would you be the kind who leaned on his shovel half the day and dug the holes only three feet deep instead of six? Or the kind who yelled at kids who cut through the cemetery on their way to school? Would you be the kind who chopped worms in half with a shovel when he came across them? Or the kind who placed them gently on the dirt pile?

It also bugs me when people say, "You're the spitting image of your father," or "You certainly are your mother's son." It sounds as if you and your mom or you and your dad are *exactly* the same, which you're not. It also sounds as if you don't have any choice about it, which you do.

From now on, people who ask me what I want to be when I grow up had better be ready to hear about the Skeet Waters Golden Moon Menu Method of Growing Yourself Up. The way it works is this. You make columns headed with the names of people you admire. If you feel like it, you can add people you don't really *know*, but know *about*, like maybe Abraham Lincoln or Mother Teresa or Tiger Woods. You can even put in characters from books or movies, as long as the characters seem real to you. Animals are okay, too.

So you write down the names, as many as you want. Then, under each person's name you write traits about him or her that you have observed. You can't use boring adjectives such as "nice," or "bad," which don't really mean anything. You *can* use groups of words. For example, under the name Abraham Lincoln, you might put "read lots of books, even though he had to walk far to get them and there was hardly enough light in his log cabin to see," which explains what you mean better than the word "determined," although, now that I think of it, that's a perfectly good word and you could use it if you wanted to.

You write down bad stuff about the person, too, if there is any bad stuff.

So you have your columns with people's names at the top, and characteristics about them under their names. Put together, the columns represent the Great Menu of Life. It's sort of like the menu at the Golden Moon Chinese restaurant, which is right here in Chassacoochie Springs. Your plate, when it's full, represents the person you want to be someday. It's a combination plate. You get to pick the things you want and skip the things you don't want.

At the Golden Moon, you can only pick one thing from each column, but since this is real life, you get to pick as many as you want. If you don't want anything squirmy on your plate, it's up to you. You are the customer and the customer is boss.

Here's how I would do it, just as an example. Two people I admire are my Memaw and a guy named Dirty Dan. Memaw—now, there's somebody I hope to be like when I grow up, so I would choose a lot of traits from her column to put on my plate. She has what she'd probably call "a talent for happiness." She is funny and honest and a real good singer.

Dirty Dan—well, he's a great fisherman, which I also plan to be someday. There are a lot of other good things about him that I would choose, like he's brave and patient. And he tries real hard to take care of his son, who has something wrong with his brain and needs somebody to watch out for him.

His son is a person I admire, too, along with his dog, because they're always together, and that's one of the good things about them, the way they're loyal to each other, and happy doing dumb stuff together.

Even in people you admire, you might notice some bad traits. For example, Dirty Dan has one real bad habit. It causes lots of problems in his life. That habit of his would be listed in the column under his name, but I wouldn't put it on my plate.

See how it works? If you make the right selections from the Great Menu, you end up being the person you want to be—not your mom or dad or grandparents, or even your heroes, but just the right combination of all of them. I recommend my Golden Moon Method. Try it.